Ready for Love
Erin O'Reilly

Ready for Love

Erin O'Reilly

Affinity
eBook Press
NZ
2016

Ready for Love
© 2016 by Erin O'Reilly

Affinity E-Book Press NZ LTD
Canterbury, New Zealand

1st Edition

ISBN: 978-0-947528-17-1

Editor: JoSelle Vanderhooft
Proof Editor: Alexis Smith
Cover Design: Irish Dragon Designs

Acknowledgments

This story was a labor of love. It would never have seen the light of day had it not been for the encouragement and story suggestions when I got stuck if JM hadn't been there. Her astute insight and helpful suggestions helped bring the story to light. She was also there to do the beta edits for me.

Thanks goes out to Affinity eBooks for taking a chance on me and my story.

Thank you Nancy (Irish Eyes) for creating a fantastic cover. You rock!

A big thank you to the editing team. Jo, you made Ready for Love a better story with you input and line editing expertise. Alexis, your proof editing was, as always, spot on. Lisa, thank you for catching all those pesky typos.

A special thanks goes to Alice who came to my rescue and made sure that every 'i' was dotted and 't' crossed.

Dedication

For Dorothy

Table of Contents

Also by Erin O'Reilly

Return to Me
If I Were a Boy
Through the Darkness
Deception
Fearless
'55 Ford
Fractured
Revelations
Wolf at the Door
Sandcastles

Writing with JM Dragon

Take Me As I Am
Against All Odds
Earthbound
When Hell Meets Heaven Series
New Beginnings
Atonement

Chapter One

"Bye, sweetheart, see you this afternoon." Kylie Wilcox waved good-bye to her daughter, Ryan, who peered out of the school bus window before it pulled away.

After a brisk walk to her home a half a block away, she crossed the lush, green grass to the gray-brick sidewalk, then walked up two steps before going inside her two-story Garrison colonial home. She had one thought on her mind coffee. She grabbed her mug off the kitchen table, headed for the percolator she'd recently purchased, and poured the dark, rich Columbian coffee into it. She closed her eyes, relishing in the warmth that flowed around her mouth before trickling down her throat.

"Today is the day I find a job." She made her way to the kitchen table with her mug in hand. After pulling out an oak chair and sitting, Kylie opened her tablet and began perusing the available jobs to see if there were any that piqued her interest.

Life certainly had become complicated after the death of her husband, Ted. Immediately after graduation from the

University of Texas, she had married her high school sweetheart. He was ambitious, and the speed at which he climbed the corporate ladder had many calling him a fast burner—and he was. Because of his success and position, he insisted she function as the perfect corporate wife. She had argued on many occasions that she needed to have a job and use her education, but once she became pregnant, the question of her working became moot. Therefore, she spent the next seven years playing the role of wife, then mother, fundraiser for charities, bridge player, and doer of all things domestic.

For a few months after Ted's death, Kylie memorialized him and their marriage as nothing short of perfection. Then, reality set in. She knew the marriage was marginal at best, for Ted cared and thought more about his job than of his daughter or wife. She also realized what she had long suspected: that orgasms were mythical and the stuff that great love stories, songs, and poems were made of—nothing more. She had no experience other than with Ted and reasoned that if she ever did have an orgasm—which she doubted—then all the hoopla was an over exaggeration. In all the time they were married, she never experienced even the slightest twinge of pleasure or excitement while making love.

Her fingers twisted hair the color of wheat and she saw her gray eyes reflected back at her as she scanned the job listings. Kylie's brow furrowed when one item caught her attention. She'd seen the same listing a month earlier for an assistant in the archaeology department at the museum. "They must be getting desperate. Maybe I have a chance. After all, the curator is a personal friend of mine, and if I stretch things a bit, I could say it is sort of in my line of expertise." She laughed, for her experience consisted of several summer outings during her time at the university. She gazed at the clock and noted it was already half past nine. Certain that someone would be there, she snatched her cell phone off the table, tapped in the number, and engaged its speaker.

"I haven't spent all these years volunteering not to be able to call in a few favors," she said as she listened to the phone ring.

"Dr. Ludlow's office. This is Ruth Smith. How may I help you?"

"Hi, Ruth, it's Kylie Wilcox."

"Oh, Kylie dear, how are you doing? I think of you every day and pray you are getting on well."

"Thank you, Ruth. I'm making the best of it and am trying to get my life back on track."

"God bless you. I don't have the assignments yet for the volunteers, but I will call you as soon as they're ready."

"Thank you." Kylie paused briefly, working up her courage. "Ruth, I noticed a job listing for the museum and was wondering if it had been filled yet."

"Oh." Ruth cleared her throat. "I take it you're inquiring about the one with Dr. Evans in archaeology and not the janitorial one. Right?"

Kylie laughed. "I get enough of the janitorial work at home."

"I understand that sentiment." Ruth laughed too. "We are still interviewing for that position. Are you interested?" Her tone sounded disbelieving.

"Yes, I am. I need to do something, Ruth. From what I read online, this sounds like the perfect job for me."

"Hmm. Okay. Kylie, can you give me a minute, please? I'm going to place you on hold."

"Certainly." Kylie's heart rate increase as she waited.

It was crazy to think she should work or that anyone would actually hire her. After all, Ted had left her financially sound to the point that she'd never have to worry about money or how she'd pay for Ryan's college. She heard the phone click and swallowed hard.

"Kylie, can you be here at eleven? You can interview with Dr. Ludlow, then with Dr. Evans, who you'd be working for."

"Wow! Eleven. I didn't expect anything that soon."

"I'm sorry, dear, it is the only appointment we have when they both are available until late next week. We do want to fill the position as quickly as possible."

"Okay. No problem. I can be there. Thank you for giving me the opportunity, Ruth."

"You're welcome. I will see you then. Oh, don't forget to bring your résumé."

"I won't. Bye, Ruth."

"Bye."

Kylie ended the call and dashed up the stairs two steps at a time. She was sure she had plenty of time, but she wanted to budget it in case anything unusual might occur. Her main objective was to make certain everything was perfect before she left. Tearing off her clothes, she headed for the shower.

†

Kylie arrived at the office of Dr. Robert Ludlow, the curator of the history museum, right on time. She knew the teal linen suit she chose to wear accentuated her eyes, making them appear grayer. She was confident that her hair was perfectly coiffed and her makeup was subtly flawless.

Ruth greeted her with a bright smile. "Hello, dear. It

is so good to see you. My, don't you look lovely in that suit."

The butterflies and the third cup of coffee where churning in her stomach, so all Kylie could manage was a smile. Ruth was a wonderful woman and a close friend with a heart of gold, but at that moment that didn't matter. "Thank you."

"You're right on time. Dr. Ludlow instructed me to show you in when you arrived. Will you come with me?" Ruth got up from her desk, motioned for Kylie to follow, and knocked on the partially open door. "Go on in. He's expecting you."

"Thank you." Kylie walked into the office and heard the door close behind her.

Rob Ludlow was all smiles and took no time in rising to greet her. "Kylie, it is so nice to see you looking so well. How are you holding up?" Once he was face-to-face with her, he engulfed her in his arms.

Kylie returned the hug. "Rob, thank you. As I told you and Louise last week at dinner, I have good days and bad ones, but at last I think there are more good days." She felt safe with Rob's arms wrapped around her.

Rob Ludlow was a tall man, not only in stature but in reputation. He was in his early fifties, trim, handsome by most standards, and kind to everyone. He was a no-nonsense, hands-on curator whom everyone at the museum and in the community respected. Kylie had met him five years earlier when she started volunteer work in the museum's gift shop. Soon she had become close friends with him and his wife, Louise. "Come, sit down, and tell me why you're interested in this job." He led her to a comfortable leather chair, then pulled another chair beside her.

"Well, Rob"—she shook her head and let out a small laugh—"I suppose since I'm here to interview for a job, I should be more formal." Her face turned serious. "I need to make a life for myself and Ryan. I think that means I need to do more than stay at home or do volunteer work." She sighed. "They are both worthy endeavors, but I need normalcy, and so does Ryan. I feel so useless, Rob." Tilting her head, she added, "I think I'm qualified for this job."

Rob patted her hand and smiled. "Did you bring a résumé, Kylie?"

Kylie frowned. She knew this would be a problem. "I brought my high school and university transcripts. Unfortunately, Ted never wanted me to work, so I don't have a work history…not even from my teenage years. I was too into sports and Ted to have time to anything else. I know if you give me the chance, I can do the job. As you'll see, I did take extensive courses that pertain to archaeology, and I've done field work." The churning amped up in Kylie's stomach. "All my grades show I excelled in those courses."

Patting her hand once again, Rob took the papers and looked them over. "Nothing to fret about. It seems to me that you might just be the perfect fit for the job. Give me a minute to fax this down to Dr. Evans, and then we can talk further." He got up, opened the door, softly called Ruth over, and handed her the documents. "Now, tell me, do you think Ryan will be all right with you working?" He shut the door.

"Yes, I think so. As you know, my parents are supportive in helping out when they can, and I know they will be there for her when I can't."

"That's important to know. The doctor you will be working for has erratic hours, and she may require you to work odd hours too."

"Okay," she said skeptically. "Erratic? Can you give me a frame of reference? Are you talking about late into the night, early mornings, or something else?" Kylie's confidence, which wasn't strong to begin with, began to wan.

"All of the above. Not that I think she'd require it of you too, but I've known her to stay late into the night, and the janitors say she can show up as early as three in the morning." He smiled. "She is very intense when it comes to her job." He scratched his head. "I'm sure you will be a good fit."

Kylie saw doubt on his face and knew he wasn't telling her something. She wouldn't ask because she didn't want him to tell her anything that might make her interview with the museum's chief research archaeologist to be awkward.

The phone rang and Rob answered it. "Hello. Yes, Dr. Evans. Excellent. I'll send her down." Rob ended the call and looked at Kylie.

"Dr. Evans is ready for you. I have another appointment in five minutes, so I can't introduce you to her. Do you think you can find your way?"

"Certainly."

Rob took out a map of the museum, circled a room on the lower level in red pen, and handed it to her. "Ruth will show you to the elevator and key in the basement. After that, just follow this."

"Thank you."

"Kylie," Rob said as she headed to the door.

"Yes."

"I shouldn't tell you this, but as your friend, I think you need to know. You are the eleventh person to interview for this job."

"Is it the job or the doctor?" At his expression, she knew the answer and that he would say nothing more.

"You will do just fine." He gave her a quick hug before opening the door. "Good luck."

She left the office, and with Ruth in tow, she walked to the elevator that would take her to the lower level and her fate.

Chapter Two

LJ Evans spent the first years of her life in the west Texas town of Canyon where doors didn't have locks and everyone knew everyone. When she was seven years old, her father's promotion had the family moving to a small, but wealthy community just outside New York City where everything was different

As LJ entered the classroom on her first day of school, the teacher asked her name.

"My name is Lucinda Jane Evans."

The teacher replied with a sweet smile and kind voice, "Nice to meet you, Lucy, I'm Mrs. Parker. Why don't you take that seat over there?" She pointed to an empty desk in the front row.

LJ let her blue eyes pierce the teacher. "My name is Lucinda Jane, not Lucy!"

"Okay, Lucinda Jane, please take that empty seat."

At recess later that morning, other kids from her class surrounded and taunted her by saying, "Lucy, Lucy is a goosey" and "My name is Lucinda Jane, not Lucy, Lucy."

The harassment continued during lunchtime. The fact she was only seven and in a fourth-grade class didn't help.

When she arrived home that afternoon, Lucinda Jane crossed her arms and told her parents she would never return to that school. No amount of cajoling on their part would change her mind. By the next week she was enrolled in a school for exceptional children. There she thrived and made great strides intellectually. From the day she entered the school, she became LJ, and at the age of sixteen she legally changed her name. Her thick skin and aloofness remained intact until at the University of Texas she met and fell in love Holly Brown. They became friends, roommates, and then lovers inside of a year.

Holly was patient, kind, and loving. Soon she was able to break down all the barriers LJ had set up and found the way to her heart. They were both passionate about archaeology and spent many hours at the Tonkawa Indian tribe digs near the university. Holly was so full of life and so much fun to be with that LJ was certain she would spend the rest of her life with her.

They had been at the dig for four weeks, and it had been the happiest time of LJ's life. She was doing what she loved—digging in the dirt and finding treasures—with Holly by her side. She looked across the expanse of the excavation area and saw her lover in what appeared to be a deep conversation with Evan Baylock, one of their professors.

Holly's red hair fanned out from beneath her broad-brimmed hat. The sun had been brutal for the last month, and she grinned knowing that tonight when she counted there'd be a million new freckles on her arms and face. Holly was kind, gentle, and loving and she accepted LJ for who she was, unlike most people. No matter what happened LJ knew Holly would always be there for her.

"Hey, babe, whatcha doin'?"

LJ smiled. "Thinking about you and how lucky I am to have you in my life."

Holly's eyes were wide with a look of amazement. "I'm about to uncover something. Do you want to help me?"

"Holly, it's your find. I'll watch you dig it out."

"Please share this with me." Holly grinned. "I can't imagine sharing this with anyone else. I love you and want you there for my first significant find."

"You are so wonderful. Come on, let's go see what you've discovered."

Holly and LJ lay side by side on their stomachs as Holly carefully brushed away the dirt from what looked like some sort of gold object. Word of the find quickly spread, and the others crowded around them. Once the top section was finally exposed, everyone gasped at what looked like a gold fertility idol Holly uncovered.

"Here, you dig it out." Holly handed LJ the trowel.

"No, this is yours, not mine."

"What's mine is yours. Please, LJ."

"Okay. Let's see what you've got here." She took the trowel in her hand and began to carefully remove the idol.

That night with everyone gathered around the fire an animated LJ was laughing and joking with the others. She and Holly sat wrapped in each other's arms, basking in the shared glory of the find and their love.

†

"LJ, don't!" Holly squealed the next day. "I promised Gretchen I'd go with her to the river while she takes a bath."

"She can wait a bit longer, don't you think?" LJ asked as she ran a finger lazily over a taut nipple. "You know you

11

can't resist my charms," she purred.

Holly smiled while pulling the sheet up over their heads. "No, I never could."

"Holly, are you ready?" a voice called from outside their tent. "It's time to get out of bed, lazybones."

Holly laughed. "I'll be right out, Gretch. I need to get my shoes on."

LJ collapsed on top of Holly. "Don't go," she pleaded.

"Tell you what. You hold that thought, and I will be back before you know it, and we can pick up where we left off." Holly nuzzled her neck. "I'll go so fast you won't have a chance to miss me."

LJ rolled over. "I'll hold you to that, so I suggest you get a move on, 'cause I'm timin' you." Holly's closeness caused a chill to run up LJ's spine. "Hey, you want me to go with you?"

"Always my protector," Holly whispered before giving her one last kiss "We'll be fine. Go back to sleep so I can wake you when I return." She winked before hurriedly putting on her clothes and shoes.

LJ stretched her long frame out and rested her head on the fingers linked behind it. A joyful smile crossed her face. She woke with a start when she heard a commotion outside the tent and sat up in alarm.

After quickly getting up and dressing, she exited the tent and began looking around the area. "Hey, what's going on?" she asked another student, Sam, who was hurrying toward the river.

"Someone is drowning," he cried. "Not sure who it is."

LJ's mind went on full alert as she scanned the area. "Holly…." Panic set in. "She's not here. I need to find her," she whispered before charging toward the river, pushing others in her path out of the way.

Five minutes later, she saw Holly lying on the bank with Gretchen trying to resuscitate her. Every fiber of her body wanted to push Gretchen out of the way, but LJ knew she needed room to work. For long, agonizing minutes, LJ watched in horror as Gretchen gave Holly her breaths.

"What's happening?" LJ screamed.

"Hey, take a deep breath. She knows what she is doing," Ed Munsey, one of the instructors, said. "They went to get the doctor."

"She can't die." LJ wrapped her arms around her waist.

Holly finally coughed and water spewed out of her mouth, then she was breathing on her own. Once Gretchen was sure she was stable, several students carried her back to her tent.

With tears cascading down her cheeks, LJ held Holly's hand while sitting by her side. Holly's breathing was uneven, and gurgles sounded from her lungs.

If only I had gone with her. What an idiot I was to let her go without me. "God, please don't let her die."

Holly opened her eyes and smiled up at her. "LJ," she whispered.

"Holly, thank God." LJ bent down and kissed her cheek. "You had me worried. You're going to be okay. They've sent for a doctor and are getting some oxygen for you." LJ's tears fell harder. "When I saw you lying on the ground, I thought I'd lost you. God, I should have been there with you."

"Is Gretchen okay? She was pulled under, and I tried to save her."

"She's okay."

"Good, I'm glad. I was really scared for her." Holly took LJ's hand and whispered, "LJ, I love you. I'll wait for you." Then she gasped, closed her eyes, and stopped breathing.

"Help! Somebody help!" LJ cried before flying into action and straddling Holly's body. She breathed into her mouth before starting chest compressions, then stopped for a moment, watching for Holly's chest to rise. It didn't. "Come on, baby, wake up and tell me this is all a nightmare."

The tent flap flew open, and a man she didn't know came inside. "I'm a doctor, let me help," he said.

"She can't die. Please save her." LJ watched in stunned silence as he tried to revive Holly. *She can't be gone. She was just speaking to me.*

"I'm sorry. If we were in a hospital, it would be different. She's gone. It was too much of a strain on her heart."

And just like that, LJ was once again alone in the world. The loss of Holly hurt so much that she vowed never to let another in. Her work became her compensation for her empty life.

†

The summer's dig in Peru was a great success. Because of LJ's status as a leading expert of the Wari' tribe they were allowed to bring some of the artifacts back to the US. LJ returned with a treasure trove of relics, the likes of which she had never seen. To her great dismay, her assistant of five months had quit, leaving her to fend for herself. She interviewed many people but never could quite find the right person who had a good work ethic and would do as she instructed. LJ didn't think that was too much to ask, but Rob had other ideas when he approached his earlier that morning.

"Listen, you're not going to get anyone to work with you if you're so hard on them when they come in for an interview," Rob said.

"I will not have some lazy ass work for me, Rob. All the applicants you've sent me think this is a no-brainer job. They are either stupid, don't want to do the work, or both. I will not work with people like that, so I will keep interviewing until the right one comes along. My research is far too important to trust it to some idiot looking for a free ride."

Rob shook his head. "Did it ever occur to you that you've spent so much time with the dead and in the past that you've forgotten how to be human? LJ, you are not going to find anyone if you treat them like you did your last assistant. Can't you try a little kindness?"

"Look around you. Plenty of people here don't have a problem with me."

"Only because they have no direct contact with you."

"Then replace me, Rob. I doubt you'll find anyone more qualified."

"I see your ego is intact. I guess that's a plus."

"Look, I've dedicated my life to this job and deserve your respect," LJ snapped.

"You have my respect—you always have—but you need to work on your people skills."

"Rob, I know what I need in the way of an assistant, and I am the one who should make that decision. Ideally, I should insist on a room full of helpers."

"We can get some students from the university if you'd like."

LJ glared at him. "There's no way I'd let a room full of kids touch anything. I'd prefer to do it myself, but that's impossible. And since we don't have the resources to give me my own staff, I've agreed to have one helper."

"You're too generous. Listen, I have a meeting with a potential candidate at eleven, then I'll send her down to you. You be nice. This one could be just what you need."

She watched him walk away and muttered, "Like you have any idea about what I need."

When the fax of the applicant's résumé arrived, LJ looked it over quickly. "Wilcox. Hmm. Sure, Rob, someone with no experience is exactly who I need." She shook her head while placing the paper on her desk before resuming her work.

†

Kylie walked down the long hall along the marble floor, looking at the room numbers until she found the correct one. The door was open, and she knocked on the doorframe before calling out, "Dr. Evans?"

From deep in the room, a strong voice replied, "Over here."

She walked in the direction of the voice, navigating the maze of shelves and bins until she saw a tall woman with dark hair braided down her back. The desk she was sitting at looked so old that Kylie was certain it had many stories to tell.

"Dr. Evans?" Kylie smiled as she approached. She tried her best to sound casual in an effort to cover her nervousness. The woman was dressed in jeans and a gray t-shirt that hugged her body, but not in a sexy way. Inwardly Kylie chuckled when she saw the shirt had a dinosaur on it with the words *dem bones dem bones* written under it. Since the doctor was the chief research archaeologist for the museum, Kylie had expected her to be much older. Instead, she guessed the woman to be in her mid-thirties and was impressed. *She must be really good at what she does.* Kylie thought about her woefully unimpressive résumé and knew she wouldn't get the job even with a good recommendation from Rob.

The woman nodded. "Mrs. Wilcox, take a seat and we can get started." She pointed to a chair next to the desk and gave Kylie a once-over, and Kylie thought she was sizing her up as she would an archaeological site. The no-nonsense tone of her voice diminished Kylie's usual positive attitude.

"Certainly," she said haltingly. She sat down on the hard wooden chair, folded her hands in her lap, and crossed her ankles.

The doctor shuffled the papers around on her desk before looking at Kylie. "I have your résumé here somewhere."

Kylie laughed nervously, thinking the doctor might be the typical absent-minded professor.

"Ah, here it is." Dr. Evans looked quickly over the document, then sighed before her gray eyes fixed on Kylie. "Tell me, Mrs. Wilcox, do you feel like a falling star?"

"I'm sorry. I…I don't know what you mean."

"This résumé of yours states that you were valedictorian in high school and graduated cum laude from UT, then nothing after that. You apparently had a bright future that faded."

Kylie couldn't believe the doctor had actually said that to her. "I consider taking care of my child a bright future," she said defensively.

The doctor raised an eyebrow. "I see you took extensive courses in archaeology and even did some field work. Can I assume you know about cataloguing and the care of antiquities?"

Kylie warmed to the question. "Yes, I spent several summers in Mexico unearthing Mayan ruins. I learned a great deal about documentation, the proper handling and the restoration of finds. It is tedious work, but the rewards are worth it." Kylie looked at Dr. Evans and smiled. "You need to be a good puzzle person."

The doctor nodded and scratched her forehead before frowning. "I do have some troubling issues that I feel need answering before I can even consider you for the job."

"Okay. What do you want to know?" The sinking feeling she had earlier increased.

"You have a child."

"That's right. A daughter."

"If the child gets sick, can I expect that you will need to take time off to be *mommy*?"

"I don't think that is an appropriate question, Dr. Evans." Kylie scrunched her eyebrows. It was easy to see why no one would want to work with this woman.

"I need to know if I can count on you being here, Mrs. Wilcox. The work I am doing is extremely important and I need reliable help, therefore my question is applicable to this interview."

Kylie considered the words and realized it was, after all, a legitimate question. Her never having had a job meant Dr. Evans would have no way to determine her work ethic. "Of course, I understand. My parents, who live here in town, are supportive, and if my daughter is ill or has school days off, I am certain they will take care of her. As to my work habits, I have done extensive volunteer work, and you are more than welcome to call the coordinators and ask how reliable I am. I never missed a day."

The interview proceeded, and Dr. Evans made no

comment on her answers. Kylie did her best to field the questions honestly, wondering if the woman had a heart of ice since she wasn't in the least bit pleasant.

"What does your husband think of your working?"

That question also seemed to be out of order, but Kylie answered it nonetheless. "He died eight months ago. It's just Ryan and me now."

"I see. Have you decided to start working so you can find yourself another man and then quit the job?"

Kylie could not believe her audacity. "How dare you ask me that question, Dr. Evans. Not only is it inappropriate, but it really is none of your business. I'm done here." Kylie stood and headed back through the maze of shelves to the door before slamming it behind her. "What an arrogant bitch!"

✝

When LJ heard the door close, she smiled. She couldn't help but notice how attractive the woman was. She was slender with shoulder-length, blonde hair, but she certainly wasn't a classic beauty. Her mouth was wide, her cheekbones high, her chin had a slight cleft, and even though Kylie's hair covered them, LJ could tell that her ears stuck out. In spite of that, the woman was strikingly good-looking with a great body to match. Her smile was one of those that lit up a room, and LJ found the familiarity of it disconcerting.

She was certainly better-looking than any other assistant LJ had had, but she wouldn't let that influence her. There was no way LJ would handle her delicately or show her any mercy. If she was right for the job, she'd have to earn it. Not wanting to give anyone the upper hand, LJ would play her cards close to her vest.

She liked the way the woman answered each question honestly and succinctly, challenging only when necessary. Her composure and reticence under fire impressed LJ. If the woman had answered her last question in the same manner, LJ knew she would have found an assistant. She needed to know why the woman's bright future faded away when she married.

To LJ's way of thinking, the husband could have been the only reason. She noted the woman's address and wondered why she wanted a job since the neighborhood in which she lived was definitely upper-class. After thoughtful contemplation, she asked the next most logical question. Was the woman there looking for a new husband?

She hadn't expected that the woman would walk out on her. No one had ever done that before.

"I do believe I have found the perfect assistant." She picked up her phone and dialed Rob's office.

"This is Dr. Evans and I need to speak to Dr. Ludlow," she told Ruth who answered.

"He's not in his office at the moment. I will connect you with his voice mail and you can leave a message, Dr. Evans."

"Fine." LJ was annoyed that she couldn't speak directly to the curator. When she heard the beep, she said, "Rob, it's LJ. Listen, I think Mrs. Wilcox is perfect for the job, so why don't you go ahead and hire her. Call me when you have all the particulars worked out."

†

Kylie's shoulders stiffened as Rob called out to her as she reached the exit "Kylie, wait up. How did it go?"

Kylie flashed the man a scathing look. "I can see why

she hasn't found anyone to work for her." The sight of her friend made her anger abate somewhat, though, and her body relaxed and the tone of her voice softened. "Rob, thank you for giving me the opportunity to interview for the job. It was a good learning experience." She closed her eyes in resignation. "Maybe I'm kidding myself in thinking I could work at a real paying job. After all, I have no experience." She shrugged. "Once I start volunteering in the gift shop again, maybe we can have lunch together."

Rob took a long, deep breath. "She can be difficult. I am sorry it didn't work out, but don't give up on trying to find a job. As for experience, I think all the volunteer work you do counts as that."

Kylie laughed. "Rob, there's nothing for you to be sorry for." She shook her head. "I think I sealed my fate when I just left."

Rob growled. "Unacceptable! I cannot allow anyone to be so intimidating and offensive that someone interviewing for a job in my museum feels the need to walk out."

"Rob, it could be that I irritated her. You know yourself that I can be rather blunt at times. Ted would always say I could aggravate a saint if I put my mind to it." She let out a small laugh.

"It is still unacceptable, Kylie. It makes the museum look bad, and I can't have that. I think it's time I have a talk with Dr. Evans."

Kylie glanced at her watch. If she didn't get going, she'd be late meeting her friends, Lynne and Jodie, for lunch. "Rob, thank you for giving me the chance." Her eyes flicked to her watch again. "I need to go or I'll be late for an appointment. Will you please tell Louise I will call her later this week?"

"Of course I will." Rob smiled. "Maybe we can get together over the weekend."

"I would like that. Sorry, but I really do need to go. I'm late. Thank you again for the opportunity to interview for the job." As she left, Rob headed down the stairway toward the basement. "Serves her right." She shook her head. "I can't believe I defended someone so obnoxious."

†

No more than ten minutes after she called Rob, LJ once again heard rapid footsteps coming her way. When she looked up, LJ saw Rob and thought he'd received her message. As he got closer, however, the look on his face told her this wasn't going to be a friendly social call.

Rob stood in front of her desk with his arms folded and a scowl on his face.

"Did you get my message?" she asked.

"What message?"

"The one about wanting to hire the Wilcox woman."

"You want me to hire her?" Rob stared at her with a perplexed expression.

"Yes. She impressed me, and I think we would work well together."

"Excuse me? Are you talking about the woman that felt the need to walk out of her interview with you?"

LJ frowned. "I need an assistant, and although she's not highly qualified, she was willing to stand up for herself, and I liked that. So what's the problem?"

"Exactly what makes you think she'd want to work for you after you browbeat and intimidated her?" Rob shook his head and leaned over the desk so he was eye to eye with her. "That is absolutely unacceptable, Dr. Evans."

LJ shrank back a little when he used the word *doctor*. "Look, I don't need this aggravation. What I do need is an assistant I can count on. The work I do is tedious and sometimes downright boring, but for me, the rewards outweigh all of that. I knew I wanted to hire the woman after her first reply, but I needed to have all my questions answered." She took a breath, trying to collect her thoughts enough to make her words sound convincing. "I needed to know how far I could push her in order to know if she's up for the job. I must say she passed with flying colors in all areas." She pursed her lips. "We both know I'm not the easiest person to work with."

"That's an understatement and still doesn't change the fact that she walked out and you made no attempt to stop her. Do you have any idea how bad that makes this museum look? Frankly, I'm not certain she even wants to work for you now."

LJ realized early in life that sometimes it was necessary to eat humble pie to get what you wanted. "Rob, you're right, I was way out of line. Would you like me to call Mrs. Wilcox and apologize? I really want her to work with me."

"No, let me do it. I'm not sure she would welcome your call. I'll get back to you with her reply." He began to leave, then turned back to face her. "LJ, we've known each other for a long time, so I feel I can say this.... Holly is gone."

LJ put her hands over her face. "Rob, I know she's gone. It's been fifteen years, but I still wake up and look for her." She looked at him and shook her head. "When she died it left a hole in my heart that runs so deep it can never be whole again."

"I understand," Rob said softly. "But you're shutting

everyone out and letting life pass you by. Don't lock yourself away anymore. The LJ I know is a wonderful woman who is caring and kind."

"I think you have the wrong person."

Rob shook his head. "We both know I don't. Give yourself a break. You have so much to offer."

"There's nothing left to give."

"Let it go and join the world of the living."

"I'm happy where I am."

"Suit yourself." Rob turned and left.

He closed the door behind him, and LJ pursed her lips. "He doesn't know what he is talking about. How could he?"

Chapter Three

Kylie slammed the heel of her hand against the steering wheel as she drove away from the museum. "Who the hell does she think she is? How dare she ask me those questions?" Ted had told her often that she was well suited for volunteer work to help the needy and that the grind of a daily job wasn't something she could handle. What did he think running a household, raising their daughter, and all the damned volunteering was if not a full-time job? Her anger continued to boil over as she braked for another red light.

"Why is it I get every one of the damn lights whenever I'm in a hurry?" Kylie ground her teeth while waiting for it to turn. The downtown traffic seemed heavier than usual, and all she wanted to do was see her friends. They would commiserate with her about the interview and the horrible woman who had subjected her to such humiliation. Her attention turned to the melody of her cell, and she pressed the hands-free button. "Hello."

"Kylie, this is Rob. Is there any chance you might consider turning around and coming back here? I have a job proposal for you."

"Rob, the last thing I want is for you to force me on her." Irritation bubbled up at the thought of him putting her in a position where she might have to grovel.

"No. You don't understand. *She* told me she wanted to hire you."

Kylie shook her head. "Hold on a minute, Rob, the light just changed." She maneuvered through the intersection at Congress and Sixth and had to stop again for the backed-up traffic. "I'm back," she said. "Listen, it was clear to me that she didn't think much of me or my life choices, so why would she want to hire me?"

"Please, just come back, get the forms from Ruth, fill them out, and then meet with both Dr. Evans and myself. Please, Kylie, I am telling you the truth."

Kylie took a moment to weigh the pros and cons of working with someone like Dr. Evans. "To be honest, after meeting her I don't know if I can."

"I understand, and if after a week you are still haven't adjusted, you can quit and I will find you another job. You said you needed to change things for you and Ryan, Kylie. Dr. Evans is giving you that opportunity. What do you have to lose?"

Kylie considered the truth behind the words and realized that if she were going to branch out, she'd have to take opportunities when they came her way. "Okay. I guess I could give it a try for a week," she said reluctantly. "I won't be able to return for at least two hours. As I told you earlier, I have an appointment I must keep first."

"Okay. Come directly to my office when you get here."

After hanging up, Kylie said, "Call Lynne" and waited for an answer.

"Hi. Are you on your way?" Lynne asked.

"Lynne, I got the job."

"Kylie, that's wonderful! You'll have to tell us all about it when you get here. Hurry, we're famished."

"Traffic is horrible. Is Jodie there yet?"

"She is."

"Order me the usual and I will be there as soon as I can."

†

Fifteen minutes later, Kylie entered the restaurant and saw Jodie waving from a table in the far corner where she and Lynne were sitting. She walked quickly to the table and sat in a vacant chair. "Finally I'm here. Sorry to be late." Lynn and Jodie were her oldest friends, and she couldn't wait to share all the details of her new job with them.

"No problem. Tell us all about the job." Lynne smiled at her.

"I knew you were thinking about working but didn't know you actually had an interview," Jodie said. "Where? Doing what?"

"I called this morning and went for the interview first thing. I'll be working at the history museum in the archaeology area. Not sure what I'll be doing yet, but I expect I'll find out when I go back this afternoon."

"Interesting." Jodie sipped her drink.

"Good for you." Lynne patted her hand.

"Tell us about your new boss, and don't skip the good stuff." Jodie grinned.

"Not a lot of good stuff to tell. From what I could tell, work seems to be her number one priority, and I didn't see much of a personality beyond that. I'll have to let you know more once I start working." Kylie put her fork down. "So what is going on with you two?"

They spent the next half hour catching up.

"I have an idea. Why don't you come over for dinner tomorrow night? Isn't it poker night for the guys? Or has that changed." Kylie looked at her friends hopefully.

"No, they still get together the second Friday of the month. Unfortunately, I already have plans," Lynne said.

"Hey, why don't we go to the Rusty Nail Saturday night? I hear the band will be great." Jodie's eyes sparkled.

"I can't go then either, but Tim is going out of town on a fishing trip with his buddies the following Friday. How about we go then?" Lynne grinned. "It will be like old times."

"Sounds good to me. It's been a long time since I've been there." Kylie looked at her watch. "Sorry, but I've gotta run. I need to get back to the museum to fill out papers before meeting with the person I'm going to work for."

"Great. I am so happy for you about the job. It's time you got on with your life," Lynne said.

"You're right. It is time. Thanks. I'll call you both later on and firm up plans for our Friday excursion." Kylie gathered her purse. "Love you two. Bye."

As Kylie drove back to the museum she was happy to have such supportive friends. Lynne was right. It was time to move her life forward.

†

LJ's phone rang, and she stopped what she was doing to answer. It was Rob. "I hope you have good news for me," she said.

"You're in luck. She's coming in to fill out the forms after a meeting she needed to attend. I'll call you when she gets here."

"How long?"

"I'd guess a couple of hours at the most."

"Did it ever occur to you or her that I might be busy in a couple of hours?"

"I'd suggest that if you want her to work for you that you be available when she gets here."

"Fine."

"I'd lose that attitude too, LJ. You're skating on thin ice as it is. I've tolerated your bad manners because I'm aware of your situation and have given you leeway. It won't last much longer. Is that clear?"

"No attitude. Check."

"That isn't helping."

"It's the best I can do."

"I expect you to be pleasant and kind. If you need an assistant as bad as you say you do, you will be on your best behavior when you meet with her."

"I don't appreciate you speaking to me like I'm a child."

"Then stop acting like one."

Rob hung up before LJ could reply. "I'll give him pleasant." Her forehead creased. She didn't care whether the woman was happy or not. All she wanted was someone to do the work and not bother her with anything personal. Yet from the moment she'd lain eyes on the woman, something about her drew LJ in, and that was disconcerting. She rubbed at her neck where tension was building.

I wonder if I'm making a mistake. Maybe I should have held out for some lackey from the university that needs credits. The thought made her cringe. She'd have to put up

29

with grad students invading her space in preparation for the next dig, and that was sacrifice enough. The Wilcox woman was a far better choice.

LJ was lost in her research when her phone rang again. "Hello. Okay, Rob, I'll be right there." She slid off her stool before heading quickly upstairs.

†

When she entered the outer office, LJ saw the Wilcox woman sitting near the door, and she felt uncharacteristically out of her element. She didn't know what to do other than take a seat and wait. When the woman smiled at her, she again realized just how stunning she was. Her linen suit hugged her taut body nicely, and the color accentuated her eyes. LJ couldn't tell if they were blue, green, gray, or a mix of the three. She knew she was on thin ice with Rob and wondered if she should say something, but she eventually decided to remain silent.

While waiting, LJ realized that if she continued to be cold and uncaring toward the woman, she'd most likely not be working for her. In order for the woman to accept the job, LJ knew she'd have to make the offer so attractive that turning it down wouldn't be an option. That meant she'd have to allow a softer LJ to come out, and she didn't know if that persona still existed.

Kylie looked at the doctor sitting across from her. Now that they were no longer in the dark basement, she looked different, and Kylie noticed how remarkable her looks were and that Dr. Evans had the most brilliant blue eyes she'd ever seen. As much as she didn't want to, she

30

smiled and was disappointed when LJ didn't return it.

The uneasiness between them didn't last long as Rob entered and motioned for them both to come into his office. Once inside, they all sat down around the smaller of the two tables in the room, making it impossible for Kylie to sit anywhere but next to or across from Dr. Evans.

"Mrs. Wilcox, thank you for coming back," Rob began. "We need to talk with you about hours and salary before you and Dr. Evans get together and work out what your job responsibilities will be."

Kylie nodded.

"Dr. Evans, how many hours would you need Ms. Wilcox to be here?" Rob asked.

LJ sat watching the woman covertly and found herself attracted to her although she was certain she didn't have a snowball's chance in hell with her.

"Dr. Evans, what do you think?"

Suddenly, LJ realized it was her turn to speak and cleared her throat in an attempt to collect her thoughts. She couldn't comprehend why she was daydreaming. She never did that.

She sighed deeply. It was time to shit or get off the pot. "Rob, I am very impressed with Mrs. Wilcox's knowledge and enthusiasm. I know we have a starting salary based on experience, and I suggest we start her off at that salary or a higher one. Also, since she has a daughter she needs to get off to school, I suggest her hours be from nine to four with a forty-five minute paid lunch." The compromising words sounded alien to her.

Rob's eyebrow raised before he cleared his throat. "That sounds good to me. What do you think, Mrs. Wilcox?"

31

Kylie was just sitting there with a curious look on her face.

"Mrs. Wilcox?" Rob said louder.

"Oh, I'm sorry. Yes, that is most generous of you both. I'm in shock. I can't believe this is happening. Thank you, Dr. Evans, for your kindness. This way I won't have to burden my parents with getting Ryan off to school or picking her up at the bus stop in the afternoon. Thank you." She was looking directly at LJ.

"Great, now that that is done, you two can head down to the catacombs." Rob got up and went back to his desk. "Kylie, when you're finished, please return to my office. If *you*"—he directed his gaze at LJ—"decide the job is indeed what *you* want to do, then you can finish the rest of the paperwork. Ruth can tell you where to go to get a physical."

Kylie nodded.

"Right, shall we go, Mrs. Wilcox?" LJ stood and started for the door.

"Sure." Kylie followed close behind.

LJ shook her head slightly at Rob's parting words. She knew he was warning her that hiring Mrs. Wilcox was not a done deal and she would need to be on her best behavior.

As soon as they were outside the director's office, the cold, uncaring demeanor Dr. Evans had during the initial interview was back in place. It made her wonder if the job, including the flexible hours and generous salary was Rob's idea rather than Dr. Evans'. This whole thing seemed ass-backward to her. Shouldn't Dr. Evans have shown Kylie what she'd be doing before she decided to work there or not?

She would make sure to ask him if she returned to his

office. In the end, it didn't really matter to her. Her goal wasn't to be friends with Dr. Evans—she already had friends—she was there only to do a job.

✝

As they entered the workroom down the hall from LJ's office, she pointed to a locker. "You can use that one for your coat and personal belongings. If you want a lock, you will have to purchase your own." She moved farther into the room. "Down here is the area where you will spend most of your time."

They arrived at a series of worktables mapped out much like a dig site. There were numerous large compartments on each table each with an assortment of bags and photographs. LJ looked over the tables. "This entire project was my idea, my study, my find, and when finished, I'm sure it will redefine Wari' history." LJ had to stop herself from gushing further. Just looking over the table and realizing the possibilities brought about an excitement that little else compared to. The previous summer's dig at a never-before-explored site had uncovered a bevy of artifacts bearing glyphs unknown to the archaeological world.

"I know my way is a bit unconventional, but I like things visual so I can recall the exact time each artifact was found. I'll need you to start by making sure everything in each compartment matches up with the catalog. After that, we'll start to recreate the pieces. I'm hoping we will be able to piece together complete or nearly complete items." She pointed to a series of shelves. "Over there are all the tools you will need for the reconstructions." She pointed to large magnifying glasses on each of the tables. "These will come in handy during the process." LJ looked at the woman. "I am assuming you are familiar with reconstructions."

"Yes, that was part of my studies. I know which gloves to use for different materials."

"Good. I won't have to stand over you to make sure you're doing the job right, then."

"No, you won't." Kylie had a rapt expression on her face. "I want to thank you for your generosity toward me. I really appreciate it." She smiled. "I can hear in your voice how passionate you are about this."

LJ wasn't used to hearing this kind of praise—particularly when it included the word *generosity*. "We shall see how grateful you are after a week, Mrs. Wilcox."

"Yes, I expect we will. Any chance you could call me Kylie? 'Mrs. Wilcox' sounds like some stuffy old woman."

LJ crinkled her forehead. What was it about the woman that made her feel disorientated? "You are here to do a job, Mrs. Wilcox, not be my friend." She ground her teeth. "I am expecting you to start as soon as possible, which means tomorrow."

"Understood. Is tomorrow around noon okay?" Kylie asked. "I have some things I need to take care of before I begin."

LJ snorted.

"Listen, Dr. Evans, I just called for this appointment at nine o'clock this morning. This afternoon I still have to fill in a stack of forms and most likely have a physical. After that, I need to make arrangements for my daughter and reorganize my life, and I can't do that overnight. I'm asking for a morning, and that isn't unreasonable."

LJ couldn't believe what she was hearing. She had gone out of her way to make sure the woman was available for her child, and now she wanted to start at her pace. She sucked in a breath and took a moment. *Exactly what do I do now? Shit, I hate this type of thing. Give me artifacts any day.* "Why don't you plan on starting Wednesday?" Her cold persona was back firmly in place. "When you get here then, park your car in the employee parking lot at the back of the building and use the entrance there. It will be unlocked. Make sure you lock it after you come inside." She didn't know what else to say and felt awkward. Being nice was not something she ever considered, yet here she was doing exactly that. "I will see you then." As an afterthought she added, "Glad you'll be working here."

Kylie blinked as the doctor turned and left. "Sure, see you then."

Dr. LJ Evans was an enigma, that was for sure. She was cold and distant, and for the most part, she never acknowledged Kylie's comments or questions. Yet, when she spoke of her work, her voice was soft, warm, and passionate. *How can that be?* She crossed her fingers that she'd made the right decision.

The comment about not being friends stung, even though Kylie had already come to the same conclusion. Ted had always told her that the workplace was no place for friendships, because when it came down to it, your colleagues would throw you under the bus in a tight situation.

She made her way out of the workroom and up the elevator to the floor that housed Rob's office. When she went inside, Ruth looked up and smiled. "I have a stack of forms ready for you to fill out." She tapped on a piece of paper. "Here is the address of a clinic for your physical."

"Is it okay if I take them home? I'd like to get the physical first so I won't have to ask my parents to pick up

Ryan."

"Certainly. I didn't expect you to fill them out immediately." She smiled. "It's a lot to take in, isn't it?"

Kylie blew out a breath, then laughed. "It's like I hopped on a merry-go-round and it won't stop. I've never had a job before."

"Not to worry, dear. Once you get into the routine, it will all make sense."

"I hope so. Is it possible to speak with Dr. Ludlow for a moment?" She bit her lip. "If he's free, that is."

The door opened, and Rob walked out of his office. "Kylie. Is there a problem?"

"No. Not at all."

"Have you decided not to take the job?"

"I'm taking it, Rob. I just wanted to speak with you. It won't take long."

Rob looked at his wristwatch. "Of course. Why don't you come on into my office?"

Kylie followed him, and when he shut the door, she turned to him. "I wanted to thank you for making sure my hours would coincide with Ryan's school day and for the more than generous salary."

Rob shook his head. "I had nothing to do with that. It was all Dr. Evans's doing."

"Really? She doesn't come across as someone who would be that thoughtful."

"I suspect that once you start working with her, you will find that LJ is a different person under the cold exterior she shows the world." Rob moved closer and gave her a hug. "It will be all right."

"Thank you, I hope so." Kylie moved out of his arms. "I'll let you get back to work, and I'll see you on Wednesday when I start."

"She didn't have a problem with that?"

Kylie grinned. "At first she did, but she finally agreed."

Rob shook his head and smiled. "Amazing. I think this is going to work out after all."

"Thanks, I hope so." Kylie left the office more puzzled than ever by the paradox known as LJ Evans.

†

Kylie didn't get to the walk-in clinic in time to be able to pick up Ryan and had to call her dad to get her from the bus stop. She parked in her parents' driveway and went to the front door carrying a bottle of chilled champagne she'd picked up on her way there. When she entered, a squeal of delight from Ryan greeted her.

"Mommy." Ryan ran toward her.

Kylie dipped down and picked her up. "Hi, sweetie, how was your day?"

"Good, Mommy. I have to make a diomama."

"Diorama." Kylie laughed

"How was the doctor appointment?" Virginia Aldridge asked as she entered the front room. "Are you sick?"

Kylie put Ryan down and held up the bottle of champagne. "I got a job at the history museum."

"Oh, I didn't know you wanted a job," Virginia said.

"What's this I hear about a job?" Kylie's father, Carl, came into the room with Ryan tagging behind him.

"Hi, Daddy." Kylie hugged him. "You are looking at the new assistant to Dr. LJ Evans."

Carl looked at his daughter, his expression puzzled. "I thought Ted left you with enough money so you didn't have to work."

"He did. It's not for the money, but for me. I can't spend the rest of my life playing bridge and doing volunteer work. I need more."

"Why didn't you come to me if you wanted to work? I still have contacts and could have gotten you a decent job."

"Daddy, this is a decent job," Kylie countered.

"You belong in an office." Carl shook his head.

"I'm sure the job is great," Virginia said, giving her husband a harsh glare. "Dinner is ready. Let's all sit down and you can tell us all about it." She hugged Kylie. "I'm so proud of you."

A few minutes later, Kylie was sitting at the kitchen table and humming around a forkful of deliciousness. "Mom, as usual, your lasagna is fantastic."

"Who exactly is this Dr. Evans?"

Kylie put her fork down and looked at her father. "She is renowned and well respected as the chief research archaeologist at the museum. It is a very prestigious position, especially for someone so young."

"How old is she?" Carl waved a fork in Kylie's direction.

"I'm not sure, but I think she's in her mid-thirties."

"What will you be doing there?" Virginia asked.

"She went to Peru on a dig last summer, and I'm helping catalog the finds and restore some of the objects."

"What about Ryan? Are you expecting your mother to take over your responsibilities?"

Kylie bristled at the comment, suddenly being reminded of Ted saying something similar.

"Carl. Enough." Virginia glared at him again. "Darling, I remember how much you loved your archaeology classes, so this sounds perfect for you."

"Yes, I agree. At one point I thought I wanted to be an archaeologist. I've often wondered what would have happened if I had pursued that career and how different my life might have been." Kylie looked at her daughter, who was happily eating a piece of garlic bread, then smiled at her mother. "I wouldn't have Ryan in my life though, so my choice was the right one."

"Yes, it was. What can I do to help you?" Virginia asked.

"They were very generous and planned my hours around the school day, so I should be good. On the days school is out or if she's sick, I'll need someone to watch her, so I'm going to look for a babysitting service."

"That's ridiculous," Carl said. "Your mother and I will do that."

"I can't ask that of you, Dad, especially now that I know you're against my working."

Carl took her hand. "I'm not against you working, sweetheart. I was just surprised, that's all."

"I know I should have discussed this with you first." Kylie suddenly felt vulnerable. "But for so many years I let Ted dictate what I did or didn't do. I needed to do this for myself."

"All he wanted to do was take care of you," Carl countered.

"No. All he wanted to do was control me."

"Surely it couldn't have been that bad." Virginia looked at Kylie with concern etched on her face.

"He took care of us, but it was always on his terms. Any time I mentioned working, he would berate me, telling me that he wouldn't allow his wife to work like some commoner. Like a coward, I gave in. I wish I hadn't." She shook her head. "I know now that I should have had more of a backbone where he was concerned."

"Grammie, what's for dessert?" Ryan asked.

Everyone laughed, and the tension in the room immediately dissipated.

Virginia said. "I made your favorite, Ryan."

"Yeah, brownies! Can I have ice cream too?"

"Of course, but first we have to celebrate your mommy's good fortune with champagne."

†

"You didn't say much about your new boss at lunch. Is he handsome and single?" Lynne asked.

Kylie, reclining on the couch and engaged the speaker on her phone as she laughed. "Hardly. It's a she, not a he, and I have no idea about the single part. I kinda doubt it. As I said at lunch, she doesn't have much of a personality."

"A woman. You're working for a woman. You know what happens when you work with women, don't you?"

"I don't, but I bet you're going to enlighten me." Kylie finally could feel her body relax. Ever since her father's lukewarm acceptance of her getting a job, she'd been on edge. Talking to Lynne always made her feel good about herself.

"Well, I of course have never personally experienced this, but I'm told that when women work together, their cycles eventually sync and it's a massive bitch fest during that time."

"Where on earth did you come up with something so ridiculous?" Kylie was laughing, and it felt good.

"My sister-in-law who works with an office full of women told me. She said they all know when not to piss each other off."

"Thanks for the heads-up. I'll keep that in mind."

"You said she doesn't have much of a personality. What does that mean?"

"The truth is I don't know. In the interview she was a hardass and asked me inappropriate questions."

"Like what?"

"She wanted to know if I was there hoping to find a man to marry."

"No. What did you say to that?"

"I walked out."

"Good for you. Wait, you walked out and she still hired you?"

"Yeah. Go figure." Kylie grinned. "I think she was desperate for someone to work there."

"So, is she a shriveled-up, old hag who gets off on spooky old relics?"

"No. I'd guess she is in her mid-thirties, and she's very attractive."

"But a bitch."

Kylie laughed. "Pretty much, but I have a feeling that's just smoke and mirrors."

"Why?"

"Because she made sure my hours would match up with getting Ryan off to school and picking her up. That doesn't gel with the bitch persona she tries to project."

"Probably not. Let's settle on a time for our night at the Rusty Nail. I can't wait to go back to our old stomping grounds and just have fun."

"Me either."

†

LJ opened the door to her apartment and locked it behind her before placing her wallet and keys on a small table near the door. Her day had been both interesting and troubling. At last, she had an assistant who she thought would do the job without needing constant direction. The disturbing part was the woman who had taken the job.

She made her way to the tiny galley kitchen, opened the refrigerator door, took out a Shiner Bock, and held the cold, dark bottle to her cheek. A vision of Kylie Wilcox came to mind, making her shake her head to dispel the image. "What's wrong with me? I was nice to her and gave her concessions I never even considered with anyone else." She took a swig of her beer. "She should have started working today, not in two days."

Disgusted with herself, she moved into the sparsely decorated living area and flopped down on the worn but comfortable dark brown leather couch. From what she ascertained about Kylie Wilcox, she was intelligent, had a good understanding of archaeology, and was easy on the eyes, which in itself was a plus. LJ found she could push her just so far before a fiery temper emerged, and that meant she couldn't bully her as she had so many others. That in itself would be a challenge, and LJ had a feeling her new employee would be up to whatever she threw her way.

LJ stood and let out a low growl. "I know just where to go to get what I need." Cassie was always a willing partner when she needed to rid herself of stress. Once she had a shower, she'd be in her truck and on to a night of casual sex with no strings attached. So what if it seemed that her destiny was to always be alone—that was her choice after she'd lost Holly. No one would ever take her place. She picked up the last picture taken of them together and rubbed a thumb over Holly's face. "I miss you."

42

Chapter Four

LJ had spent a restless Tuesday prowling her office, waiting for Wednesday to come. She found herself anxious about the arrival of her new assistant. The little voice that kept her emotions in check had been telling her that hiring the woman was a bad move. Kylie Wilcox had done something no one had in a long time—made her sit up and take notice. For LJ, that was disconcerting. Desperately wanting to distance herself from the woman, she decided being her usual cold and unresponsive self would do the trick.

After parking her truck in the empty, dark employee parking lot, LJ headed for the museum. She unlocked the side door, wondering if her new employee would arrive early or be the type to get there exactly on time. She seemed like the type to be early.

Not wanting to seem eager for the woman's arrival, LJ decided it would be best to make herself scarce for a while. She took a quick look around the area, and when she was satisfied all was as it should be, she left to work on a new display featuring artifacts she found in Argentina. All the while, the question concerning her new assistant kept running through her brain—*what if...?* Although she'd just met the woman, she couldn't deny the attraction. But she had made her choices, and Kylie Wilcox did not enter into the equation. All that mattered was that the woman did her job and kept her in the loop.

†

Kylie arrived at the museum a half hour early, not knowing if the door would be open before her prescribed arrival time. She was mildly surprised that it was. After she entered the building, she locked the door as instructed. Perhaps in the future Dr. Evans would trust her with a key, but she suspected she'd have to earn it and she wouldn't hold her breath. The museum didn't open until noon on Wednesdays, and the building was eerily quiet. Down the corridor, she saw a man running a dry mop over the floor. He didn't seem to take notice of her, so she punched in the code for the door leading to the lower level, and when it swung open, she headed down the stairs. Once she found her locker, she put her things inside and affixed the lock she'd bought the day before to it.

Dr. Evans wasn't in her office, so Kylie went to the large, brightly lit workroom, expecting to see her there. She wasn't. "Guess I'm on my own."

She began inspecting the items on the table. Each had an index card attached, describing the contents, the date of the find, and location at the site. A container with all the artifacts along with another card identical to the first accompanied the rest. A large envelope containing photos of the relics' actual position at the dig was also there. After she checked each section and decided where to start, Kylie became lost in sorting through the first container on the table.

"Good morning, Mrs. Wilcox. Did you find everything you needed?"

Kylie looked up and smiled. "Good morning to you too, Dr. Evans. Yes, I have everything. I hope you don't mind that I just started working."

"Yes, it is okay. Carry on."

Kylie watched her boss quickly turn and walk away. She shook her head and sighed. "She's certainly an odd duck," she mumbled before returning to the job at hand. The work was interesting, and it didn't take long for her focus to settle once again on the pieces of pottery in her gloved hand.

For the first time in years, Kylie was content with what she was doing. During her married life, she never found any reward in all the volunteer work she did or the endless committees her husband conned her into joining. In fact, she only ever felt useful when she was with Ryan. Now as she tried to unravel the mystery of something centuries old, she felt alive in a way she never thought possible. Despite working with a dour woman, Kylie was happy to be there. She would manage the stoic Dr. Evans just as she always had in the past with people like that—with professional courtesy.

Not for the first time, she wondered if Dr. Evans had a life outside the museum. How had such an accomplished woman become so cold and heartless? She suspected it was a coping mechanism; now, she would have to figure out what she was coping with. The possibilities were endless, but with time and careful observation, she'd find out.

She pulled one of the large circular magnifying glasses over and held a sliver of pottery under it. "I know where that piece goes." Kylie picked up the clay pot she was working on and used tweezers to gently place the fragment where it belonged.

✝

Midmorning, LJ called a nearby small restaurant and ordered a sandwich and salad for delivery by eleven forty-five. She didn't fully understand why she then walked quietly to the workroom and stopped at the doorway to watch her latest assistant at work. The woman was completely engrossed in what she was doing and didn't even notice her standing there. LJ again realized just how attractive she was, but something else was drawing her to the blonde. LJ shook her head to rid herself of these feelings before leaving as quietly as she arrived.

Once she was back at her desk, the image of Kylie sitting at the table methodically doing her work kept reappearing. She immediately put the longing out of her mind. "Don't even go there." She went back to the task at hand, knowing that immersing herself in her work was the best way to get rid of unwanted thoughts and feelings.

A voice from the door called, "Delivery."

"Over here." LJ watched a young kid who looked like he was twelve walk lazily toward her.

"I got an order for LJ. Is that you?" he asked.

LJ nodded. She took the bag and noticed the him looking at her expectantly. "I already paid and added a tip. Is there something more I need to do?"

"No. Thought I'd wait and see if you got the right order."

"Are you telling me that the people you work for are so inept that they can't get a simple order right?"

"No, ma'am. They tell me to make sure the customers are satisfied."

LJ opened the sack and saw a salad in a clear plastic container and a wrapped sandwich. "Everything is good."

The kid didn't move.

"You can go now."

Once the boy left, LJ took the bag and walked briskly toward the workroom. She stopped next to the worktable, amused that her new assistant was so engrossed in her work that she didn't even look up.

She instantly regretted being there. She'd told herself being nice and providing lunch on the first day was a way to ensure that Kylie would keep working for her. Now she questioned that decision. Deep in the recesses of her mind, she knew there was more to her gesture than being nice. Nice wasn't what she did. She cleared her throat.

Kylie lifted her head with a puzzled look on her face.

LJ held out the bag and made her best attempt at a smile. "Time for lunch. I didn't know what you would want, so I have a turkey sandwich and a salad for you." When Kylie looked at her in bewilderment, she asked, "Don't you like it? I had them put all the condiments on the side. There are three choices of salad dressings."

"No. I mean, yes. I do like it. I just didn't know it was lunchtime already. Let me get my wallet out of my locker and I'll pay you."

Confusion rattled LJ's brain. "You don't need to. This is a benefit of the job. Paid lunch means the lunch is paid for too." Uncomfortable and once again feeling like a square peg in a round hole, LJ looked away. "I'll print out the menu for you so you can tell me what you'd like each morning."

"Thank you. I lost track of time."

There was that smile. LJ had a hard time keeping herself from trying to smile in response. She placed the bag on a nearby chair. "There is a table over there where you can eat. I don't want the artifacts contaminated with food." She walked toward the worktable. "Have you found any discrepancies? My team of grad students arranged all of this after we got back from Peru last summer."

"None so far. This is so fascinating. I was holding something that someone hundreds of years ago held, and it blew my mind." Her eyes widened. "I remember the first dig I was on. I found a grinding stone with the rock used for grinding nearby. I couldn't even begin to describe how amazing that felt. I bet you feel that way all the time."

Uncomfortable, LJ looked at her feet.

"I'm sorry for rambling like that. It's just that I'd forgotten how incredibly exciting archaeology is."

"Yes, it is." LJ fought the urge to settle in and have a conversation about what she'd found over the years and how she felt about those discoveries. "It also involves a lot of tedious work."

"It does, but the rewards far outweigh that. Do you know anything about these artifacts yet?"

LJ cocked her head and actually let a genuine smile curve her lips. "I'm sure you know that the Incan Empire was the largest empire in pre-Columbian America. The Wari' tribe predated them."

"I've heard about them. Weren't they into agriculture and at their peak had an immense empire? They were a remarkable civilization," Kylie added.

"Yes, that is right. I'm certain there are many Wari' villages such as the one we found still waiting for someone to discover them. Once we assemble these fragments, we will know more about this particular Wari' tribe." LJ picked up a piece, held it in her hand, and inspected it carefully. "The jungles of Peru hold many secrets. It is just a matter of finding them and deciphering the clues." She let her eyes scan the table and waved her hand at it. "Any one of these items might hold the key to unlocking the mystery that surrounds an entire civilization's disappearance." She pursed her lips. "Of course, they didn't disappear completely since most of the people in Peru today are Wari' and Incan descendants." She heaved a sigh. "The empire itself, though, was lost."

"I find this all so exciting. I can remember as a child finding a cache of arrowheads with my grandfather. I was hooked then."

LJ found her assistant's enthusiasm refreshing, and she stood there uncomfortably. Her plan was to deliver the lunch and leave. Instead, she wanted to spend the day talking with the fascinating woman about archaeology. But that wouldn't be acceptable. "Hope you enjoy your lunch, Mrs. Wilcox," she said in her coldest voice before turning and leaving. All sorts of red flags were waving, telling her to keep away even though part of her desperately wanted the contact.

Kylie sat in confusion as she watched the doctor walk back to her office. She would have remembered if an actual lunch was included in her job description. Now the sandwich she'd made along with Ryan's that morning was sitting in her locker and would go uneaten.

She was certain her new boss was uncomfortable with her being there. When she spoke of her work, though, she was relaxed and engaged, and her voice changed from cold and impersonal to warm and enthusiastic, showing her passion for the subject.

A slight smile curled her lips. She knew that given the opportunity she would have happily spent the day just listening to the melodic sound. "Like that'll ever happen." She grabbed the bag off the chair and opened it, pulled out the contents, and heard her stomach rumble. She was suddenly famished.

The sandwich was excellent, and she appreciated the thought of putting all the condiments on the side. Often, turkey sandwiches came slathered with mayonnaise, and she preferred only a small amount. The salad was a mix of spinach and kale, and although she'd never tried that combination, she found it very tasty, especially with the addition of strawberries and mango.

If that were the caliber of food she'd have every day, she'd always look forward to lunchtime. Of course, that meant she'd get to spend more time with her boss, and she found herself smiling at the thought. With trepidation, Kylie mused over the thought of getting to know more about Dr. LJ Evans. *I wonder what LJ stands for? That might be the beginning.*

✝

The next day LJ arrived in the workroom with Kylie's lunch in hand and sat it on a stool before looking over Kylie's progress.

"How am I doing so far?" she asked.

"You've only been working for a day and a half, and that isn't enough time to make any sort of judgment on your capabilities," LJ said with what sounded like uncaring stiffness. "But so far it seems as though you have a grasp of what is needed. Time will tell if that will warrant praise."

Kylie couldn't help thinking that she'd somehow offended her boss. *I should have just kept my mouth shut.* The last thing she wanted to do was give Dr. Evans a reason to fire her. "Thank you for the lunch."

"It's what you ordered, isn't it? A roast beef wrap and a kale-and-spinach salad along with a bottle of water."

"Yes, that's correct."

LJ turned to leave, then spun back around. "Just give me your order for tomorrow before you leave today so I can order it when I arrive in the morning."

"I know you're busy, so I can do the ordering so you won't have to," Kylie offered.

"It comes out of my discretionary spending budget, so I must do it."

"Okay."

"If you want to take a break and eat outside, there are picnic tables outside the back door that I've seen other employees using."

"Yes, I saw them yesterday when I went out to stretch my legs. Thank you." Kylie watched LJ walk back to her office, then stood, picked up her bag and drink, and headed out the door. Perhaps the other museum employees could give her some insight about her boss.

†

When Kylie came to the picnic table, a short, round woman said, "Well hello there." A woman with bleached hair who looked to be in her sixties was sitting next to her. "I'm Marie Wilkerson, and this is Corrine Barber. Marcus Dunleavy should be joining us soon." Marie smiled warmly. "Take a seat. You must be Dr. Evans's new worker bee."

Kylie sat down. "I'm Kylie Wilcox, and yes, I work for Dr. Evans. How did you know?"

"Bless you," Corrine said. "She's had so many people come and go over the years that I've lost count. Nothing gets

51

by us oldies." She grinned. "Besides, we all received an email along with your photo saying you'd been hired. Poor Sally Johnson who worked for her last year would go home every single day crying. She finally had enough and quit. I'm glad because I thought she was going to have a nervous breakdown."

Why is she telling me this? Kylie looked at the two women and frowned.

"The woman is a heartless bitch at the best of times," Corrine added.

A tall, dark-haired man sat down next to Marie and smiled at Kylie. "Hi, I'm Marcus Dunleavy. You must be the new assistant in archaeology."

Kylie smiled. "Yes." She held out her hand. "Kylie Wilcox."

"Pleased to meet you," he said, shaking it. "I bet you're all talking about the resident witch."

Everyone but Kylie laughed.

"Do you all remember Jack Tremble? He was a really nice guy, but that woman managed to run him off in less than two months," Marcus said.

"I heard she hates everyone and goes around at night changing displays to her liking." A small, younger man slid into the seat next to Marcus. "Hi, I'm James O'Malley. I hope you have a thick skin."

Kylie took a bite of her sandwich that LJ had ordered and paid for. What these people were saying about her boss didn't compute with what she'd seen so far. Although LJ did come across as cold and had behaved inappropriately during Kylie's interview, she certainly wasn't heartless or dispassionate. *That certainly isn't a dispassionate bitch.*

After listening to other museum gossip for about five more minutes, Kylie rewrapped the rest of the sandwich she'd taken a bite out of and put it back into the bag with her salad. "It was nice meeting you all. I need to get back to work."

"She won't give you more than fifteen minutes for lunch? You're supposed to get at least a half an hour." Corrine frowned and looked at her with expectant eyes.

"I get forty-five minutes, but my work is so interesting I'm anxious to get back to it." Kylie turned to leave.

"She'll take advantage of you if you don't take all the time you're allotted," Marcus said.

"Don't worry. I can take care of myself." Marcus made an additional comment that Kylie didn't hear as she entered the building. She decided that she'd listened to all the horror stories about her boss she cared to hear. One day was enough to solidify her decision to take lunch inside by herself from then on. From her limited knowledge of LJ Evans, Kylie knew the doctor would never allow any of those people to get close to her, and she resolved to break the mold and get to know who her boss was.

"I can't believe that those people spoke about her that way," she muttered to herself. "Who do they think they are? They don't even know her. Jerks!"

Chapter Five

After eight days, Kylie had fallen into a suitable work routine that was not only satisfying but interesting beyond her wildest expectations. Her interaction with Dr. Evans was practically nonexistent. When she brought Kylie's lunch to her, Dr. Evans would occasionally take the opportunity to give her some information about the particular object she was working on at the time. Other than that, LJ's usual cool and distant personality stopped Kylie from trying to speak with her.

She recalled trying to engage LJ in conversation the day after eating outside with the other employees. As always, she was friendly and respectful when she asked where LJ had gone to school. LJ only shook her head before turning and walking away. After that, Kylie kept her replies to yes, no, and okay, keeping her focus on her job and not her boss. She finally accepted that LJ Evans was never going to be anything more than what she was—tight-lipped.

It was now Friday, and the week had gone by quickly now Kylie had found a rhythm to her work. While waiting to hear the familiar footsteps enter the room, she thought about the upcoming evening with her friends. While she was married, her friends had often asked her to go on a girls-only night out, but Ted always came up with a reason for her not to join them. Now that he was gone, she realized how much she'd given up, and the irritation she should have felt back then bubbled up now. "What a fool I was," she mumbled.

"What did you say?"

Kylie looked up to see LJ's blue eyes gazing at her in question. "I didn't hear you come in."

"Obviously." LJ sat the now-familiar lunch sack on a stool before walking around the table. "Any problems?"

"Everything today seems straightforward."

LJ picked up one of the artifacts and inspected it. "I see you made some progress."

"I did. As you can see, that piece"—she pointed to on the one in LJ's hand—"is a vase. It was so exciting when I put the last piece in place and found that it was all there. Does that happen often?"

"It depends on the site and whether it was looted or the elements and time took a toll. I remember one place where everything we found was in pristine condition." LJ shrugged. "That is the exception rather than the rule."

"That must have been so exciting for you."

LJ bent slightly to look at the pottery. "There's that glyph again."

"Is it significant?"

"To the Wari' it was. It is the Staff Deity, a god associated with the sun, which they worshiped. This one is holding a staff in each hand, which is normal for this figure. What isn't normal is the sun above the image. The ones we've found have a sun around their heads." She raised her eyebrows. "I've never seen it depicted like that before."

Kylie smiled at her. This was the first time LJ had had a meaningful conversation with her. "That is incredibly interesting. Should I expect to find the Staff Deity again?"

"Yes. They used it on their pottery and textiles."

Kylie moved so she was standing next to her boss.

LJ straightened, took a step away, and nodded. "Enjoy your lunch."

Kylie could hear the warmth in her voice but it became cold indifference before LJ turned and left her without so much as a *see you later*. Every time she thought the doctor was thawing, LJ seemed to close down and walk away. Kylie shrugged and pulled the sandwich out of the bag. In a little over four hours, she'd be heading home to get ready for the night out with her friends.

†

LJ closed the door behind her when she entered her office. She needed to create a barrier between herself and Kylie Wilcox. Over the last week, she would often find herself standing in the doorway of the workroom watching Kylie concentrating intently on what she was doing, apparently unaware that someone was watching her. Each day lunch would arrive and her stomach would do a flip at the thought of taking the bag to Kylie. It was becoming harder to keep her distance and not interact more. Often she'd find her mind wandering to the workroom and the woman there and would have to squelch the feelings the image evoked.

"Why did she have to stand next to me?" she asked the empty room. Kylie's perfume was intoxicating, and whenever LJ smelled it, she became lost in pure desire. Her body's reactions to the woman were unacceptable, and her efforts to control them weren't working. She was unnerved by how easy it would have been to sit and talk with Kylie all afternoon about the Wari' tribe. Instead, she'd made a hasty retreat, but not before seeing the look of confusion on Kylie's face.

She felt a pang of guilt about inflicting that kind of emotion on Kylie. When she'd realized after working with Kylie for two days that she was attracted to her, LJ's first inclination was to fire her. But if she let her go, she would need to give Rob a plausible explanation, particularly because she had no actual complaint about Kylie's work.

"I need to take myself out of the equation," she reasoned. "The only problem with that is I need to work with her and teach her." It was a no-win situation. LJ had gone through enough assistants to know what a find Kylie Wilcox was as an employee. She had no choice. Somehow, she would have to control her ever-increasing attraction to the woman.

She looked at the clock. If she resisted going back into the workroom for another four hours, Kylie would be gone.

The afternoon flew by. Before she knew it, LJ heard, as she did every afternoon, her new assistant scurrying down the corridor on her way out of the building.

LJ was restless. "I need to get laid," she muttered. "That'll do the trick."

†

Kylie hurried home so she could get ready to go to the Rusty Nail with her friends. She'd already arranged for her parents to pick up Ryan from school and keep her overnight, and Ryan was excited about spending time with them. Ryan could always count on her grandmother baking chocolate chip cookies and her granddad setting aside time for a playdate. Kylie, meanwhile, could count on her doting parents letting their granddaughter get away with things her mother would never allow.

After putting the finishing touches on her makeup, she looked in the mirror and smiled. She was happy to go out with her friends, especially since she'd always had to find an excuse not to spend time with them when Ted was alive and her new job had renewed her sense of self-worth and given her a purpose outside of what had become her comfort zone. She reveled in this newfound freedom in spite of the enigma of LJ Evans.

Kylie had to admit working for the woman wasn't a bad thing. She was puzzled to find something about LJ compelling in a way no one had ever interested her before. For all of her adult life she made plans and rarely veered off the course she had set. Now she found herself wanting more than to do her job and go home. She wanted to get to know LJ Evans, and that did not fit in with her neatly constructed plans for her and Ryan's life. Her mind wandered back to the dinner she'd had with Rob and his wife several nights earlier.

"How do you like the job so far?" Rob had asked her.
"I like it very much."
"And, Dr. Evans…is she treating you okay?"
Kylie saw Rob's concerned look and nodded. "Yes, she does. Tell me about her. She seems awfully young to be the museum's chief research archaeologist."
"In case you hadn't noticed, she's brilliant, and like most very intelligent people, she's a bit quirky."
Kylie laughed. "She is at that. What's her

background?"

Rob shook his head and rubbed his eyes. "My position at the museum demands that I not gossip about the employees. I will tell you that she's a very private person, and I doubt you will ever get her to open up."

"I wasn't gossiping, I just wanted to know more about her."

"I know." Rob patted her hand before handing her a glass of wine. "If you want to find out more, why don't you look her up on the Internet?"

Kylie snorted. "I already did that and found very little. I would have thought there'd be more, given what a high-profile job she has."

"Some people just don't want to share their lives that way."

Kylie looked in the mirror one last time. "I've wasted enough time trying to figure her out. She obviously wants anonymity. So be it."

The phone rang, and she hurried to answer it.

"Hello. Kylie, am I interrupting?" her mother asked.

"Hi, Mom. Is everything okay?"

"Yes, dear. I just wanted you to know we picked Ryan up, and she convinced her granddad that we needed to have dinner out."

"Don't tell me. You're at Sonic and she's having chicken strips and tater tots."

"Exactly. She's even talked your dad into a getting her a chocolate milkshake."

Kylie laughed. "I guess junk food once in a while is okay."

"You don't mind?"

"No, not at all. She loves being with you guys."

"Have a great time tonight. You deserve it."

"Thanks, Mom. I'll see you in the morning."

"Good-bye."

"Bye." Kylie ended the call and smiled. She stepped into the garage, pressed the door opener, and got into her car. "Tonight is going to be fun."

✝

Lynne, Jodie, and Kylie went to The Rusty Nail Dancehall, which had been one of their favorite haunts during their years at the university. Entering the place was like going back in time—swinging saloon doors opened to a room with a twenty-foot mahogany bar complete with brass rail, spittoons, and a large mirror with a tantalizing nude painted on it. A dozen tables surrounded by chairs filled the room. Another archway led to the dancehall, which had numerous long tables and benches in the middle with others lining the side of the room. There was a large stage at one end with a dance floor in front of it. In another section against the far wall were two pool tables. The band, a group called Cassie and the Cassettes, was setting up against the wall on the other side of the bar. A section cut out of that wall allowed the bartenders to pass drinks through to the dancehall for the waitresses to pick up.

Lynne returned from a trip the bar and placed three bottles of beer on the table. "Wow, this is great. It's just like old times, isn't it?"

"Know anything about the band that's playing tonight, Lynne?" Jodie asked.

"I heard them play when Tim and I came here a few months ago. They have a decent sound, and the lead singer can really belt out a song. I think they're probably regulars." Lynne laughed. "Guess you will find out for yourselves soon enough." She nodded toward the area where the band was going through a sound check.

Kylie's heart hummed with excitement. "This place hasn't changed at all since I was here seven years ago." She grinned. "I can't remember the last time I went out just for fun. With Ted, it was always about being where everyone would see him, and he wanted to rub elbows with all the right people. This"—she waved around the room—"is my kind of fun. I love it, and it still looks like a great place to people-watch."

"I'm glad you decided to come with us, and you're right about people-watching. See that guy over there?" Lynne pointed to a man who was about six feet tall with brown hair that was obviously a toupee. He was dressed in jeans and t-shirt and had a bulging beer belly. "I've seen him here before. He thinks he's God's gift to women and hits on them all the time. Never gets lucky though." Kylie and Jodie laughed, and Lynne joined them.

"Look at that guy over there; now he's a hunk. Want me to see if we can fix you up, Kylie?" Jodie asked.

Lightly slapping Jodie, Kylie shrieked, "Noooo," before laughing again.

"How is the job going? Do you like it, Kyl?" Lynne gently touched her hand.

"I love it. It's so interesting…." She pensively stared off into the distance.

"What's the matter?" Lynne asked. "That look tells me you're regretting something. Do you think you made a mistake taking on a job?"

Kylie looked into Lynne's eyes. "No. Not a mistake. I just can't figure my boss out. But I will. You know me. I can always charm them in the end." She smiled, then gave her friend a quick hug.

"Hey, guys, look over there at the table near the door. Every time I've been here, I've seen that woman sitting in the exact same place. She usually drinks a few beers and then leaves. Oh, look, the stud man is going to try his luck with her." Jodie was laughing again.

Kylie looked at the man, who was straightening his back and attempting to suck in his beer belly. She watched as he walked in the direction of the doorway, and when she saw the woman he was heading toward, her jaw dropped in surprise. LJ Evans was sitting at the table. When the man approached her, Kylie could tell by the way she was acting that his advances annoyed her—she'd seen the look before. She watched in fascination as LJ's cool exterior turned to ice as she rebuffed him.

"You go, girl!" exclaimed a laughing Jodie. "Looks like Stud Man lost again. I can't believe he actually thought someone like her would have anything to do with him."

"What do you mean by 'someone like her'?" Kylie asked.

Jodie grinned and shook her head. "Kylie, look at her. She's gorgeous and classy, and he's a big, fat slob. Do the math. Duh. I thought you were the brainiac."

"You graduated where, Kyl?" Lynne's words brimmed with laughter.

Kylie looked in her boss's direction again. There was no denying that LJ Evans was attractive—*beautiful* was a better word. She had noted that fact when they first met, but seeing her in this setting made it all the more obvious. "You're right, she is way too good for that guy." She looked at her friends. "I can't believe it. She's also my boss."

"Get out. You can't be serious," Jodie said.

Kylie raised her eyebrows. "I wonder why she's here."

"Probably for the music." Jodie took a swig of her beer.

"She's definitely not how I pictured her," Lynne said. "I thought she'd be in khakis with a vest, boots, and a fedora." She pointed her beer bottle in LJ's direction. "I'd never guess the woman sitting over there is a renowned archaeologist."

"She certainly doesn't fit the stereotype," Jodie added.

"No, she doesn't." Kylie looked at her friends. "Do you think I should go say hi?"

"You said she wasn't particularly friendly, Kyl, so going up to her might not be a good idea." Lynne shrugged. "Just sayin'."

Kylie nodded in agreement as the band took to the stage to begin their set. Cassie, the lead singer, looked every bit the part. Her spiked, short hair was green, she had pierced eyebrows, and when she opened her mouth and held a long note, Kylie could see the piercing on her tongue. As it should be, the other three members of the band were rather bland in comparison. But when Cassie started to sing, her smooth and mellow sound made the listener forget all about her appearance.

"Wow! Are they great or what?" Jodie shouted over the music.

Every now and then Kylie glanced over to where LJ was sitting and weighed the wisdom of going over and saying hello. If LJ saw her there and she didn't say something, it might look bad. But the idea of speaking with LJ in such a different place than work was strange, and she felt out of her element. This was a night out with her friends, and LJ Evans didn't fit into that equation.

When the band took a break, Kylie decided she should approach LJ first on the off chance that she'd seen her there. "My turn to buy, who wants another?" she asked her friends. "I think I should stop by and say hi just in case she saw me."

"You're probably right." Lynne held up her bottle. "I'll have another one."

"Me too." Jodie grinned. "Good luck."

Kylie wove her way through the crowd as she headed to the bar and was surprised when LJ came into view again. The singer was leaning into her in a provocative manner. Kylie squinted, wondering what was going on, and finally it dawned on her. She moved forward but the crowd made her stop when she was opposite LJ. It appeared she was getting up to leave with the singer, and at that moment blue eyes turned in her direction. Kylie looked away in embarrassment and made her way to the bar, where she got the bartender's attention and placed her order for three beers. Several of the band members were standing next to her, and she found it difficult not to overhear their conversation.

Back at the table, Kylie gave her friends their drinks and shook her head. "Did you see my boss and that singer?"

"No," Lynne and Jo answered simultaneously.

"A couple of the band members were at the bar talking about it."

"What did they say?" Lynne asked.

"Basically that it looked like the singer was gonna get lucky and after the break they'd only be doing love songs. One of them said there was pure desire in my boss's eyes. Since she and my boss went outside together, I figured they are going to…." She looked away. "You know."

Jodie scrunched her eyebrows together. "I would think the songs are prearranged."

Lynne shook her head. "Duh! You aren't listening. Kylie's boss and the singer are going to make out or maybe more."

"She's gay! Yuck. Kyl, did you know that?" Jodie asked.

Kylie shook her head.

"Hey, there's nothing wrong with being a lesbian," Lynne said. "If I recall correctly, a few of our sorority sisters were lesbians."

"Oh, I know and I don't have a problem with it really...it's just...I don't know...." Jodie shrugged. "I'm just being silly. Everyone has a right to live the life they want, but it just isn't a lifestyle I'd choose. Life is too difficult to add something that not everyone accepts to it."

"I don't think it's a conscious choice, Jo." Lynne took a long swig of her beer. "What do you think, Kyl?"

"Who you love isn't a choice," she said petulantly.

Jodie held up her bottle. "To love." They clinked their bottles together. "I love this place. It has so many interesting people."

"Hey, look over there. That guy is hitting on someone else." Lynne laughed. "Think he ever gets lucky?"

Jodie laughed too. "If he does, it's just wrong."

Kylie listened, trying to ignore the nauseous feeling in her stomach. It had to be the beer along with the fact that she hadn't eaten since lunch.

"Is everything okay? You don't look so good." Jodie put an arm around Kylie's shoulders.

Kylie didn't know what to say because she couldn't even explain what she was feeling to herself. "Yeah, I'm fine. I guess I'm just not used to the nightlife anymore. What do you say we get a snack?" She let out a small laugh. "I forgot to eat before I went out." She shrugged. "Too excited about tonight, I guess."

"Chips and queso?" Lynne asked.

"Sounds good." Kylie's eyes strayed to the door. "Want me to get it?"

"Nope, I've got it." Jodie waved at one of the waitresses and placed the order.

Fifteen minutes later, the band was warming up, but the singer wasn't there. Finally, she hurried back into the room, looking disheveled. Her shirt was cockeyed, and if it was at all possible, her hair was messier than earlier.

"She looks like she had a quickie during the break." Jodie wiggled her eyebrows, then laughed. "Guess what you heard was right."

They all turned their heads and watched as the singer picked up the mic and with a smile began to sing.

"Well if the sultry song she's singing is anything to go by, it must be love." Lynne touched Kylie's hand. "What do you think?"

"I think she must be a slut." Kylie couldn't keep the vehemence out of her voice.

"Tell us how you really feel." Lynne was regarding her with concerned eyes.

Kylie looked over to see if LJ had come back inside and frowned when she didn't see her.

"Kyl, are you okay?" Jodie asked worriedly. "It's not like you to judge someone so harshly."

Kylie ran a hand over her face. "I'm sorry, I don't know what got into me. It just seems wrong to me that she'd screw someone during the break." She laughed. "I guess I'm getting too old for this scene." She shrugged. "Maybe I'm a prude and out of touch with reality."

"No, you're not. I'm with you, it really is in poor taste," Jodie said. "You just found out your boss is gay, Kylie. Are you going to keep working there?"

"Of course I am. I don't care about who she dates. It's none of my business."

For the rest of the night, Kylie couldn't get the image of the singer pawing at LJ out of her mind. The vision just kept playing in one continuous loop, and she was relieved when her friends suggested they call it a night.

†

LJ parked her truck and walked purposefully toward the Rusty Nail. It was exactly where she needed to be for some sort of distraction from her unruly thoughts. Once inside, she nodded to the bartender, who handed her the usual Shiner beer, then she proceeded to the dancehall and sat at a table just inside the doorway. As she looked around at the Friday night crowd, she immediately saw Kylie. How could she miss her? Ever since the blonde's arrival the week before, LJ couldn't get her out of her mind. It was almost impossible to concentrate or stay focused at the museum. Often she'd pace among the relics trying to get a handle on her agitated feelings before Kylie showed up for work.

The fact she couldn't seem to escape Kylie even here was a problem, but she was determined to ignore her A feral look crossed her face as she took in the band.

A slob of a man approached her. "Hey, baby, good to see you here tonight. Can I buy you another one?"

"Get lost," LJ said without even looking at him.

"Why don't you come sit with me, honey, and I can show you a really good time." He was leering at her, his breath stale with beer and cigarettes. He grabbed himself and winked at her before reaching out to touch her.

LJ grasped his balls and squeezed them hard. The man's face turned red as he grimaced in pain. "I said get lost!" She gave one last hard squeeze before letting go.

The man turned and walked away while awkwardly covering himself in what looked like an effort to stop the pain. She watched him leave, then looked at Kylie Wilcox sitting with two other women. When the band began playing, LJ looked away and took a long swallow of her beer before turning her attention to Cassie, aroused and in need of relief. Soon she was lost in the music and thoughts of what was to come. Still, she was unable to stop from looking over at Kylie. When the band took a break, LJ saw Cassie heading her way. *Yep, she's just what I need.*

"Hey, lover, glad to see you here tonight." Cassie leaned in to LJ. "Mmmm, you smell so good." She rubbed her body against LJ's legs as she bent to whisper in her ear. "What do you say we get out of here? I can't wait to feel you inside me."

LJ was on fire, throbbing with desire as she felt the woman's hot breath in her ear. She gazed over the singer's shoulder and saw Kylie looking at her. She growled as she grabbed Cassie's hand, then led her quickly outside and to her truck. Once inside they embraced in a flurry of passion as hands began groping and touching.

Stopping Cassie's advances, LJ whispered, "No, let me." Then she ripped Cassie's shirt aside and closed her mouth around the taut, waiting nipple pierced with a ring. She grabbed the gold circle with her teeth and tugged until the singer squealed in delight. LJ moved her hand under

Cassie's skirt and was pleased there were no panties to deal with. She jammed her fingers deep inside Cassie before pumping her hard and fast. It was just what she needed—an impersonal, mind-blowing fuck.

The singer's move to get her face between LJ's legs had LJ lowering her jeans and underwear before leaning back and spreading her legs. Cassie trailed kisses down her body, and once she reached her goal, LJ grabbed her head and held it there. "Harder. I need it harder."

Cassie came up for air. "Mmmm, you take my breath away, lover. You like the feel of my tongue ball against your clit, don't you?"

LJ could only grunt as she too gasped for air. The effect the tongue piercing had on her drove her to distraction. She needed that relief from the tension she'd been feeling over the last week all because of that blonde assistant who even now was invading her thoughts. Suddenly she wondered what the hell she was doing there. Was this really what she wanted?

Cassie closed in on her again, but LJ pushed her away. "Don't you have some singing to do?" Her voice was cold, distant, and laced with loathing.

The look on the singer's face said she knew there wouldn't be any more interaction between them tonight. "You know one day you're going to want me and I am going to say no."

"That will never happen and you know it. Now run along," LJ sneered and pulled her jeans up before zippering them. She slid across to the driver's seat, put the key in the ignition, and started the truck. Staring coldly at the singer, she raised an eyebrow. "I said go."

Cassie got out and walked away, and LJ slid the gearshift backward and started down the street. She gave the bar one last glance before heading into the darkness alone.

Chapter Six

She'd had a restless night and kept waking up. After making her way to the bathroom, she stood at the sink and splashed water on her face. "Must have been overstimulated by all the noise, music, and beer." Her reflection in the mirror knew better. "Yeah, right." She knew exactly why she couldn't sleep, and it had nothing to do with noise or beer and everything to do with her boss. Seeing LJ with the skanky singer triggered something in her that she didn't understand. The image of LJ leaving with her arm wrapped possessively around the woman kept her tossing and turning all night.

It was the first time since Ted's death that she'd come home to emptiness and been overwhelmed by the significance of that. The thirty-two-hundred square foot house seemed even more cavernous than it had at any other time. A pang of loneliness enveloped her, and she had to fight the desire to race to her parents' house and get her daughter. Now that it was light, she could take a shower and show up at her parents' without having to explain why she was there so early. It was only six thirty, but they were early risers, and with her conflicted emotions swirling in her head, Kylie needed to see Ryan and hold her close to ground herself.

✝

The morning air was crisp and cool as Kylie stepped out of her car. She smiled, knowing that when she entered, she'd find her mother in the kitchen making Ryan chocolate chip pancakes.

Her shoulders relaxed as she walked through the front door. It was where she'd grown up and was the only place she truly felt safe. Ryan came out of the kitchen, squealed, and barreled into her. Kylie scooped her up and held her close. "Good morning," she whispered into Ryan's blonde hair. "Are you having a good time?"

"Yes. Grammie is making me pancakes."

"With chocolate chips?"

"Well, this is a surprise." Virginia poked her head out of the kitchen, then moved toward Kylie. "I thought you'd take advantage of the alone time and sleep in."

Kylie gently released Ryan and hugged her mother. "It was way too quiet for me." She ruffled Ryan's hair and smiled. "Alone time is overrated, and I missed Ryan's chatter." Her face heated. "I wanted to come at two, then again at three, but made myself stay home."

Virginia nodded. "When you went to camp, it was like one of my arms had been severed. You're just in time. I just flipped the last pancake."

"Right now I'd kill for a cup of coffee."

"I have that too."

Kylie followed her mother into the kitchen and gladly

took a cup of what she knew was rich, strong coffee. She looked at the table that held pancakes, bacon, and eggs before laughing. "Is there an army coming?"

"No. It's what Ryan asked me for."

"Mom, you spoil her. She would have been happy with cereal."

"That's what grandparents do." Carl walked into the kitchen, pulled out the chair next to Ryan, and gave her a hug. "Ready for breakfast, sweetheart?"

"My stomach wants food," Ryan said. Everyone laughed.

They fell into a companionable silence as they began eating.

"So how was your night out?" Virginia asked.

Kylie put her fork down and chewed on her lip. "It was interesting and fun. Any time I'm with Lynne and Jodie it's a good time."

Virginia eyed her daughter and nodded.

"Mommy, Grandad is going to help me make a birdhouse."

Kylie smiled. "I remember when I was about your age he helped me make one. I think I painted mine red."

Ryan looked at him. "Can I have a yellow one?"

"I think we can do that." Carl smiled at Kylie. "Do you have the time for us to do it after breakfast?"

"Of course. I always love being here."

"You know that the offer still stands." Virginia patted Kylie's hand. "You two can move back here with us."

"I know, Mom, and I've thought about it, but if I do that, then it will be like going backward. I took the job so I could move forward."

"Well, if you ever change your mind...."

Kylie squeezed her mother's hand. "I know and I

appreciate it."

Ryan put down her fork and looked at her granddad.

Carl smiled. "Are you ready to build that birdhouse?"

Ryan jumped out of her chair and grabbed his hand. "Yes!" They quickly exited the kitchen, and Kylie smiled at the sound of her daughter's endless chatter.

"So what's going on?" Virginia asked once they were alone.

Kylie knitted her eyebrows. "What do you mean?"

"What happened last night that's got you all tangled up in knots?"

"Mom...."

"A mother knows these things. I always have. Spill."

Kylie looked around the warm, inviting kitchen and drew in a breath. "We had a great time. It was more noise than I'm used to, but being with my two best friends was wonderful."

"Okay, I already knew that. What else?"

"I saw my boss there."

"Dr. Evans?"

"Yes."

"Did you speak to her?"

"When the band took a break, I started in her direction, but by the time I got through the crowd, the singer was with her and it looked like they were getting rather chummy."

"I guess that wasn't the time to say, 'Hi, how are you,' was it?"

Kylie closed her eyes, recalling the incident. "No, it wasn't."

"Was he a nice-looking guy?"

"That's just it...it wasn't a guy."

Her mother's mouth formed into an O. "Did she see

you?"

"Just as I passed by, I looked at her, and she was staring at me, and now I don't know what to do," Kylie confessed.

"Why? I remember in high school you were good friends with um…. Carol Kieslowski, and she was a lesbian, wasn't she?"

Kylie nodded.

"You're not a homophobe, so what's the problem?"

"I don't know if she's out or not. Rob never said anything about her being gay, and the few people I've spoken to didn't mention it, and believe me they would have. What if by my seeing her there, I unintentionally outed her? What do I say to her when I see her on Monday?"

Virginia put her arm around her daughter's shoulders. "You say, 'Did you have a good time Friday night? I know I did,' and leave it at that."

"It's going to be awkward, Mom."

"Only if you make it that way. Just go with the flow and see what happens." Virginia nodded at the table. "Let's get this cleared away and make some cookies."

Kylie looked at her mother, and her heart filled with love. Throughout her life, her mom had always given her sound advice and was usually right. She hoped this time wouldn't be any different.

†

LJ lay on her back staring at the ceiling early the next morning. The encounter with Cassie had resulted in an unsatisfactory orgasm, which was the norm with the singer. LJ only kept going to her because Cassie was always a willing participant—there was absolutely no emotional attachment on her part. Then there was her new assistant.

Why was Kylie at the Rusty Nail? She didn't belong there. LJ watched her laughing and having what looked like a good time with her friends and felt a pang of jealousy she hadn't experienced since Holly was in her life. Kylie had obviously seen her with Cassie, and unless she was an idiot—which she wasn't—she knew what was going on between them.

I wonder if she's already contacted Rob and told him she can't work for a deviant? That thought brought on a melancholy that LJ hadn't experienced since Holly's death. She couldn't deny that the entire time Cassie was pleasuring her, she couldn't stop thinking about Kylie.

"She was married for God's sake and has a kid. What the hell am I thinking?" LJ shivered and pulled the sheet over her naked body. "What'll I do if she quits?" She threw her arm over her eyes. "I've fucked this up big-time. I should have left the moment I saw her there or at least sent Cassie away. Shit, what am I going to do?"

Unable to sleep, she got up and dressed. She'd go to the museum and get lost in her relics so she wouldn't have to remember The only problem with that, however, was that she couldn't forget about Kylie there either. Kylie's imprint was all over her relics and was a part of her life now, no matter how many barriers she set up.

✝

When Monday came around, LJ once again watched and listened for Kylie to arrive. She'd been there sitting in the shadows since three a.m., and even the janitor hadn't noticed her. As the now-familiar footsteps drew nearer, her heart rate picked up while she held her breath. LJ let it out as they passed her, having assumed Kylie was heading to her office to tell her that she was quitting. She surmised that Kylie was probably just getting her things out of the locker.

A full twenty minutes passed, and she wondered when the hammer would fall. There was no way a refined woman such as Kylie Wilcox would let what she observed between LJ and Cassie go without judgment. After all, that's what most people thought about her sexual preference. *She's probably an ultra-right-wing conservative who has no tolerance for gay people.*

LJ frowned. Absolutely nothing in anything the woman had said or done indicated she had any feelings one way or the other on the subject. Still, what the woman thought mattered to her, and that fact alone was too much for her to handle. She had no reasonable explanation for her evolving out-of-control emotions, and for LJ that was objectionable. There was always a reason for everything.

Noon drew closer, and her stomach was a riot of knots in anticipation of seeing and talking to Kylie. The week before she'd tried desperately to keep her distance while longing to get close to her. With the woman's departure each day, LJ felt a pang of loss and sorrow as well as confusion and upset for allowing it. The last people who had gotten that close to her had been Holly and her grandmother. Despite resolving last Friday night not to allow her emotions to run unchecked again, she felt like an emotional mess. If only she could go back and undo what happened at the Rusty Nail.

†

Kylie arrived at work Monday morning hoping she wouldn't see LJ. She didn't think she could look her in the eye after seeing her with the singer at the Rusty Nail. Her mother had been right—she wasn't a homophobe, and what LJ Evans did in her spare time and with whom was of no concern to her. Yet when she saw the two women together, she'd had a strange feeling that bordered on wariness about the singer's intentions. LJ was way out of Cassie's league and could do so much better.

"What do I care," she said. "I barely know the woman." But for some unfathomable reason it mattered to her more than it should, and that disturbed her.

Kylie resisted going into LJ's office when she arrived. Instead, she stowed her things in her locker and went into the workroom. Her eyes widened and she gasped when she saw notes attached to many of the artifacts, and she panicked. *Has she fired me? Is it because I saw her with that singer?* Then again, LJ couldn't fire her for she'd done nothing wrong.

Swallowing hard, she moved to the table and picked up one of the notes. It read: *I think if you try to envision this as something like an urn, it will come together quickly.* She took another sticky note and saw a similar message. After inspecting each yellow square of paper, she breathed a sigh of relief. *I'm not fired.*

Kylie sat on her stool and began with the first one she saw, envisioning it as the piece LJ had asked her to imagine as an urn, and true to LJ's guess, Kylie was able to put it together quickly. The next thing she knew she heard LJ approaching her. "It must be lunchtime," she said.

"Yes, it is." LJ's voice was soft and a bit tentative.

She looked up and smiled. "I had a great time at the Rusty Nail Friday night. Did you?" She held her breath as LJ's blue eyes seemed to be appraising her.

"It was okay. Didn't stay long."

"I know. I was going to say hello, but you left. That band was great." Kylie knew she was pushing it, but if she was going to let LJ know that she didn't have a problem with lesbians, she needed to sound casual.

"Yeah, it's semi-permanent. I liked the place better when they had different bands each weekend."

"I remember going there all the time with my friends when I was going to the university. It hasn't changed at all." She met LJ's gaze and held it. "We had a lot of fun reliving old memories."

LJ gave her a long, hard stare. "Have a good lunch," she finally said.

Kylie watched her move quickly out of the room. "Well, that went better than I thought it would," she murmured when LJ was out of earshot. Her mouth watered as she picked up her lunch. Nerves had gotten the best of her, and she couldn't stomach breakfast. Now she was ravenous.

Before returning to the job at hand, Kylie made a phone call.

"Well, this is a pleasant surprise. You usually text me when you're at work," Virginia said.

"Mom, I wanted you to know you were right."

"I usually am." Virginia laughed. "About what?"

"I did what you said and told Dr. Evans I had a good time last Friday, and it seemed to break the ice. Before that she was rather hesitant."

"It pays to lay all your cards on the table. That way, you both know where the other stands."

"Good advice. Thanks, Mom, you're the best. Well, I've got to get back to work. I just wanted to let you know how things went."

"Thanks. Do you and Ryan want to come for dinner?"

"Not tonight."

"Okay. Talk to you later."

Kylie ended the call and smiled. Her mother always was her best sounding board.

✝

In the sanctuary of her office, LJ tried to digest the meaning behind the conversation she'd just had with Kylie. From what Kylie had said, it was apparent that she didn't judge LJ for her sexuality. For some reason that mattered to her more than it should, and that in itself was perplexing

LJ would be fooling herself if she denied that she was instantly attracted to Kylie Wilcox when they first met. The fact that Kylie didn't condemn her being a lesbian was significant on so many levels. She thought of Holly and the deep bond they'd shared. No one would ever eclipse that relationship no matter how attracted she was to Kylie. Holly had been her everything.

"Nothing can or will happen even if she is so inclined." The cold, relic-filled room listened as it always did without passing judgment or giving praise. Her heart became hollow, and she reined in her feelings, replacing them with the normal cold and impersonal ones—even though in the deepest recesses of her heart she cried out for warmth.

Chapter Seven

As the weeks passed, no matter how hard she tried, Kylie still couldn't get a handle on LJ or understand her behavior. She was often detached, but there were times when she actually seemed to like her. Every so often, LJ would join her for lunch, and on those occasions, Kylie found her to be affable and amusing.

On one such day, Kylie had been working on trying to fit together an intricate piece when LJ came in with lunch as usual. She set it down and began to leave.

"Will you stay and share this with me? There is plenty, and I would appreciate any help with this artifact…it's really frustrating me," Kylie said. She'd wanted to do that many times lately but never had the nerve. Her problem with the reconstruction seemed like a perfect opening.

A slight smile crossed the doctor's face as she turned back. "Come on now, Kylie, it isn't that hard, is it?"

Kylie had to catch her breath, as that was the first

time her boss had called her anything but Mrs. Wilcox. They sat there sharing a sandwich as LJ looked over the piece, then told Kylie the story of the discovery of the artifacts.

"In 2013 near El Castillo de Huarmy in Peru, archaeologists found an untouched royal tomb with sixty-three mummified women that dated to the Wari' Empire. We've talked a bit about the Wari', but do you know when their empire existed?"

Kylie chewed on her lip as she tried to recall the date. "Not sure. Somewhere around 800 CE?"

"Close. There is evidence of them existing from 600 to 1100 CE when they mysteriously disappeared." LJ fingered one of the pieces of the puzzle. "It took some time, but finally I had enough funding to go to Peru with a team to see if we could locate a similar site. "We had a plane go up to scout for ruins using techniques like oceanographers do when mapping the ocean's bottom. And we found a site." LJ gave out a small laugh. "I'm usually very meticulous, but this time I really screwed up. Why, I don't know, because it wasn't my first rodeo, but it never occurred to me just how dense the surrounding jungle was to get there. We had to hack away at thick vines to reach the dig site."

"Oh no, how long did it take you? Did you actually do the hacking or did the bearers do it?"

LJ was all smiles. "I wish. We all took turns, and eventually we came upon the identified coordinates." A look of awe came across her face. "Then we cut away some vines around what seemed to be a pyramid-type structure. A wall appeared covered in glyphs. It was incredible to view a building that no one else had seen in hundreds of years. I remember thinking at the time that it must have been the way the archaeologists felt when they opened Tut's tomb."

Her face was so serene and beautiful as she retold the

story that Kylie found herself mesmerized by the look.

"Well," LJ said, sounding uncomfortable. "I need to get back to work. Thanks for sharing your sandwich."

"Please tell me more. I heard about mummification in South America, but my knowledge is limited."

LJ looked at her with a curious expression before nodding. "Okay. The earliest evidence of mummies was about seven thousand years ago with the Chinchorros in South America. They would take out all the organs and replace them with sand, grass, sticks, and ash. There is some evidence that they sewed up the incisions with human hair. After that they covered the bodies in mud, finishing by creating a mud face mask and a wig of human hair."

"Wow. Have you seen any of them?"

"Yes. The process they used is very similar to what the Egyptians used thousands of years later."

Kylie, fascinated by the information, wanted to hear more, but LJ finally stood and left, citing the work she had to do. As she watched LJ leave, Kylie could feel the air being sucked out of the room, and she was bereft at the loss.

†

As her attraction to LJ grew, Kylie became more and more confused about what it all meant. Her mind kept tracking back to the singer hanging on LJ and kissing her. She had always admired the female form and often would look surreptitiously at women, reveling in their beauty. Kylie rationalized it as merely identifying with women since she was one. She knew her fascination with LJ couldn't be sexual and reasoned it was due to her admiration of a strong, in-charge woman. One she hoped someday to become like.

Yet, every day when LJ came into the workroom and

stood close to where she was working, Kylie's heart rate picked up. At those times, she had to concentrate on her breathing and resisting the urge to connect with LJ with a touch, if only for a brief moment.

Soon Kylie knew the sound of LJ's footsteps, the smell of her cologne, and the different variations in her voice that indicated her mood. There was no doubt that she found LJ Evans fascinating, but something else was going on. Kylie felt excited and happy when LJ was around, much as she did when she first met Ted. That was not only disturbing but enticing.

†

LJ ignored the books and notations strewn all over her desk as she tapped her fingers on the wooden surface. As always, she was listening for Kylie to leave. Then she could let out the breath she'd been holding all day, thankful she'd made it without doing something she'd regret.

She was getting dangerously close to doing just that by always standing as near to Kylie as she dared whenever she visited the workroom. Kylie was intoxicating, and on more than one occasion, LJ had had to rush out of the room when her desire blossomed to want, then need. It was at those times she knew she had to keep from doing something she would regret. She'd then hide out in her office or at one of the museum's displays to avoid Kylie.

When four thirty rolled around, she wondered why Kylie was still there. *Doesn't she need to pick up her daughter? Is something the matter?* Maybe Kylie was sick and needed attention. She was about to go and check on her when she heard the familiar footsteps. Quickly she grabbed the reconstructed bowl she'd retrieved earlier in the day and hunched over the artifact, looking at it intently.

"I'm leaving now. I think I may be on to another piece, but at the moment my eyes are too tired to focus correctly."

LJ looked up and stretched. "Yeah, that can happen. Sometimes you just need to walk away to get refocused." She gazed at Kylie's body before closing her eyes, willing her heart to slow down. When she opened them, there was that beguiling smile again, and she wanted to smile back but didn't. She took her own advice and refocused on the bowl, afraid her eyes would betray her true feelings. Once Kylie walked away, she could begin to breathe easier, and she waited for that moment.

"LJ, would you like to have dinner tonight with Ryan and me?"

Closing her eyes in yet another attempt to try to gain control and distance herself from the temptation, LJ sighed. "I can't tonight. Already have plans. Maybe some other time."

"Sure."

LJ's heart sank at the note of sadness in Kylie's voice and looked up to see disappointment on Kylie's face. The fact she was the cause of it stung in a way she'd never experienced before. Kylie had always been kind, generous, and accepting of her, yet LJ remained standoffish. She longed to get to know her since she'd never had a real friend. Maybe Kylie could be that, because anything else was out of the question.

LJ listened as the outer door closed. Sadness, an emotion she hadn't experienced since her gran died, filled her heart and prevailed long after Kylie had gone.

†

Several days later, Kylie was finally able to finish piecing together a rather complicated bowl just as LJ came in with lunch. She beamed. "Look, LJ, I have another whole one."

When LJ reached over to take it, her hand brushed against her shoulder and Kylie had to catch her breath. For a moment, her eyes held LJ's and she saw the reserve in them before dropping her gaze.

LJ took the bowl and ran a calloused finger over it as she examined the relic.

"What do you make of these markings?" Kylie asked. "They're rather odd and a bit different from what I've seen piecing other artifacts together."

"This is a strange marking, that's for sure. It looks almost like a sun symbol but not quite." LJ looked up at Kylie. "During the Wari' period and beyond, the people in the area often adorned their jewelry, textiles, and artifacts with images of winged beings going toward a door that they believed led to the sun. We've consistently seen that same theme with the Incans, Mayans, and other South American civilizations. The most interesting thing about this image is the similarity it has with the Egyptian sun god Ra." LJ fingered the piece again. "I've always thought it was fascinating that throughout recorded history the sun and stars have always been prominent in many civilizations. We see astrology components at Stonehenge, with the early Egyptians, and in all the ancient South American cultures. I don't think it's a coincidence."

Kylie leaned in closer to LJ to get a better look and pointed to an area on the bowl. "It's intact. I checked it several times to make sure part of it wasn't missing. I noticed what I thought looked like wings around what appears to be a person. Do you see that too?"

"Yes, that is exactly what it is." LJ took a step back.

"Do you think it's Wari'?"

"Most definitely. There is something anthropomorphic about this winged being."

"Are you saying that because this winged being has more human characteristics than others you've seen?"

"Yes."

Kylie cleared her throat and took a step backward, trying to put space between them. For some reason, her body was trembling. She wanted to chalk it up to the excitement of the find, but something told her it had more to do with LJ's closeness. LJ Evans was invading her thoughts, and she didn't know why.

Picking up a magnifying glass, LJ leaned in closer, and her head almost touched Kylie's. She had to breathe deeply to gather her wits. Being so near to Kylie made her senses peak, and it took all she could do not to act on her feelings. Focusing on the bowl was her only defense to keep herself in check. "I think we have a significant find here."

LJ turned toward Kylie and saw the flushed look on her face. It puzzled her, and the only thing she could think of was the temperature in the room "Is it too hot in here for you? I can have maintenance turn the thermostat down if you'd like."

Kylie flapped her hand in front of her face. "Yes, it is a bit warm."

"I will call them to turn the heat down, then." LJ pointed to the lunch bag. "I brought you a chicken Caesar salad and a strawberry smoothie." When Kylie looked at her in confusion, she asked, "That's right, isn't it?"

"Yes."

"Okay. When you're done with lunch, see what more you can come up with in the area where this bowl came from. Let me know if you find anything else."

LJ swallowed hard and left quickly. Once she was out of the room, she leaned back against the cool tiles of the wall. *Damn, what am I getting myself into?* She shook her head and muttered to herself as she returned to her office. "Get a grip and stop acting like a hormonal teenager."

Chapter Eight

Kylie had been working at the museum for almost two months now, and with each day, she found herself increasingly captivated by LJ. Most days being around the woman was almost too distracting, and she was continually trying to find opportunities to connect with her and failing miserably. In the past, she hadn't had a problem with feeling people out and making them comfortable, but LJ was the exception. It was perplexing, but she'd continue to try, knowing that eventually LJ would give in.

Kylie left work on Friday looking forward to the weekend so she could separate herself from her campaign to engage her boss. Her quest overloaded her senses in a way that was both damning and exhilarating.

Her parents were taking Ryan to visit her great-grandmother, which meant Kylie had the whole weekend to herself. She called Lynne and Jodie but neither could get away until Saturday.

After walking over the same area in her living room

for the hundredth time, she could still feel the pull of the conundrum that was LJ. She needed to get a grip. Her increasing fascination was getting out of hand, and she had no idea how to curb it or what to do next. LJ obviously only wanted her to do her job and not to become friendly, and she knew LJ would not welcome any attempted intrusion into her personal space or life. But to Kylie, that was like waving a red flag in front of a bull, and made her even more determined.

Not able to stand the quiet of her house any longer, she decided she needed to be somewhere where there was noise and a multitude of people. With that thought, she grabbed her keys and jacket and headed out the door. The Rusty Nail had been calling to her ever since she saw LJ there, and she secretly hoped to see her there again. As she got in her car, she hoped to find LJ again in a setting other than work—even if her girlfriend was there. *Maybe tonight if LJ is there she'll be alone.*

"From my lips to God's ears." She snorted at the absurdity of those words and guided her car down the highway.

†

After buying a beer, Kylie went into the dancehall area and found a seat close to the door, but not too close. She looked over at the band setting up and frowned when she saw Cassie. *Damn.* She swallowed some beer and scowled. *Stay or go?* Too keyed up to go home to an empty house, Kylie decided to stay. *I'm already here anyway. What harm can it do?*

Once the band began to play, Kylie glanced over to the table by the door where LJ had sat the last time. It was vacant. Her heart sank a bit, but the notion that the green-haired singer and her doctor weren't a permanent item cheered her. The combination of mellow songs and beer helped relax Kylie. As they played their last song of the set, Kylie decided to take the opportunity to get something else to drink before the bar became too crowded. Putting her bottle down on the table and heading for the bar, she saw LJ sitting at her usual table listening to the music. Kylie's heart jumped at the sight of her, but she kept moving. When the band stopped playing, Kylie was within a few yards of LJ. She turned and saw Cassie moving in the same direction.

Not tonight, slut. Kylie hurried in LJ's direction, only to have an onslaught of thirsty patrons engulf her.

†

It had been another emotional week for LJ. When she watched Kylie leave for the weekend, she vowed to get over her stupid schoolgirl crush. Mooning over someone who would never care about her like that was stupid and unproductive. *What's wrong with me? Lucinda Jane, you need a reality check.* She smiled, recalling her gran saying those very words to her.

Once again, she began chastising herself for her perceived weakness. The little voice inside her head told her what she needed, and she argued with it until she lost the battle.

After leaving the museum, she headed to her apartment to get a shower and then go out. She loathed herself because she knew where she would go and what she would do there. She needed release. To dominate and take so she could eradicate the barrage of thoughts involving Kylie. It was the only fix she could think of.

91

"You're a brainiac and the only solution you can think of to the problem is a quick fuck." She sat in her truck for a long time after parking near The Rusty Nail Dancehall. With her window rolled down, she could hear the mellow sounds of Cassie's voice. "You can always leave now," she whispered. Losing the battle, LJ got out and walked toward those swinging doors. For a moment, she paused, shaking her head. "You are pathetic, Lucinda Jane," she mumbled before going inside.

The crowd was thinning out as the band took its first break of the night. LJ just sat there watching as Cassie walked in her direction. The singer leaned in, her lips lingering near LJ's ear before she ran the gold ball over her earlobe.

"I thought you weren't coming back," she cooed before she bit down hard.

LJ scanned the room while Cassie was having her way with the ear. When she felt someone watching her, she knew instantly who it was—Kylie. For a moment her heart seemed to stop while she tried to comprehend why Kylie would be there.

"Hey, LJ, I thought that was you," Kylie said as she approached.

At a loss for words, LJ swallowed hard before pushing Cassie aside. "It's me all right." She felt Cassie move to her side again as if she were protecting her territory. Irritated by the singer, LJ growled, "Wait outside for me." With her heart hammering in her chest, she turned her attention to Kylie, not caring whether Cassie listened or not. "Do you come here often? It doesn't seem like your kind of place."

"And just what would my kind of place be?" Kylie countered. "I told you that my friends and I used to come here all the time in college. Tonight I was on my own, so I thought I would get out and relax while listening to the music."

"Have you been here long enough to relax?"

"Not really. I was on my way to get another drink when I saw you." Kylie smiled.

"You shouldn't be drinking and driving." LJ wanted to get away from this stilted conversation and do what she came there for—fuck Cassie and go home.

"I'm not going to drive drunk. Two's my limit. This is the second time I've seen you here. Are you a regular?"

"I'm only here when I'm in the mood." For a moment, LJ wondered what would happen if Kylie knew what that mood entailed. She slowly eyed the blonde and swallowed hard, needing to squeeze her legs tighter as pleasure coursed through her body. *Damn, this has to stop.*

"It was nice seeing you, LJ."

Kylie was turning to go, and LJ couldn't help but feel anxiety and sadness at the thought of her leaving. "If you're going out, I'll walk with you." LJ caught up with her and walked ahead of Kylie, clearing a path to the door. Her heart began racing harder when she realized Cassie was outside waiting for her. *Dammit.* But it was too late to do anything about that as the doors swung open and they walk out into the night air.

Kylie touched LJ's arm. "You can do better than her, LJ," she said as she glared at Cassie who was leaning against a car and tapping her foot.

LJ took her arm and led her to the side of the building. "I can do better? With who? You?" She didn't mean to sound so angry, but LJ was clearly out of her element and that scared her.

An expression that looked like recognition crossed

Kylie's face.

"Yes," Kylie whispered, "with me."

LJ pulled her close and kissed her deeply, running her tongue over the soft lips, which parted for her. She stopped and took a step back, glaring at Kylie. "Is that what you want?"

"Yes." Kylie put her arms around LJ's neck and drew her in for another kiss.

All the bells and whistles in LJ's head were going off, and she pushed Kylie away. "It will never happen." Inside she was shaking, afraid to let her true emotions show and terrified of what might happen if she did. "I'm not going to be your experiment for a walk on the wild side," she bit out. "Find someone else, because it won't be me."

"An experiment, you say. That's not what this is." Kylie was looking her straight in the eyes.

"Whatever." LJ shook her head. "It will never happen. I don't fuck my employees." She turned away from Kylie, who was staring at her with what looked like a startled expression and walked over to Cassie.

Once they were inside, she roughly kissed Cassie, lifted her skirt, and rammed three fingers inside her. Cassie tried to do the same, but LJ yanked Cassie's fingers away from her crotch. "No."

"Hey, no fair." Cassie went for LJ again only to have her fingers swatted away.

Cassie's orgasm came hard and fast, but LJ didn't let up. "Again, come again for me."

Cassie cried out, "Stop, you're hurting me."

Horrified and ashamed at her actions, LJ wiped her fingers on the singer's skirt, opened the door, got out, and then turned back to her. "I won't come back here to be with you ever again."

"You're a cold, heartless shit. I don't know why I got involved with you in the first place. Go on and go. I don't want you around me anymore." Cassie glared at her. "Get the fuck out of my life!"

LJ slammed the door and walked quickly away. In the lonely night, she headed for her truck, hanging her head in shame. Thoughts of Kylie, who she'd cruelly turned away, filled her mind, making her disgrace all the greater.

From the vantage point of her car, Kylie watched LJ enter the singer's vehicle only to get out a few minutes later, looking furious as she snapped at the woman in the car. It hadn't been difficult to see what was happening inside Cassie's car, since it was parked under a streetlight. Feeling like a voyeur, she chastised herself for watching the sexual encounter in fascination, unable to look away.

When LJ had asked, "With who? You?" Kylie had realized what was behind her quest to be friends with LJ—her interest was romantic. She closed her eyes, relishing in the powerful feelings of arousal the kiss caused.

"God, what's the matter with me? She's a woman. I'm a woman." But in her heart, she knew that being attracted to a woman didn't matter.

Chapter Nine

LJ looked in the bathroom mirror Saturday morning, wondering how her life had gotten so out of control. For the last fifteen years, she'd found no need to have friends or even be pleasant to anyone. All she'd needed was her work and an occasional impersonal liaison. Now she was confused, fetching lunches, and worrying about another human being.

"You have to get a grip on yourself," she said to the image in front of her.

"But how do I do that?" the image argued back.

"You suck it up and rebuild your defenses, simple as that," she countered.

"I don't want to go back to being alone."

God, I'm talking to myself now. Can it get any weirder?

A tear made its way down her cheek as she thought of how lonely her life had been since Holly and then her gran had passed away. The last time she'd cried had been at her grandmother's funeral. Now the thought of Kylie Wilcox was calling out to her heart, filling it with emotion and need. With a sudden jerk of her hand, she wiped the tear away and walked into her bedroom, where she changed into jeans and a t-shirt and put on her work boots. Once she'd gathered her dig bag from a closet, she headed for the door.

The university had a site south of the city where beginning archaeology students and volunteers who were interested in the field could dig and learn. That was where she would go. There she could center herself again and find the answers she needed. She knew the healing sun would be warm on her back as she carefully dug and brushed while explaining to the students and volunteers what she was doing. She couldn't help but laugh at the irony of looking for the past to find her future

†

"Well hello, stranger," a low, sexy voice said.

Doctor Maxine Dylan was the dean of archaeology at the university. Her taut body and shapely legs begged for attention and appreciation. Her long, auburn hair was usually pulled back into a ponytail that fit through the back of the baseball cap she always seemed to wear. She was an exceptional archaeologist and had collaborated on LJ's excursion to Peru by providing a workforce of her best students and graduate assistants. She was also at the dig as an advisor.

"Mind if I join in today, Max?"

The woman's eyes raked over her body. LJ hadn't anticipated that Max would be there. In the past, she rarely spent time at the dig site, opting to send one of her graduate students instead.

"I never mind you joining me in anything." Max ran a

finger down LJ's arm, and LJ swatted it away. "Everyone, listen up."

The participants at the dig stopped what they were doing and looked in Dr. Dylan's direction before an excited hum went through the crowd.

"Today we are privileged that Dr. Evans came here to join us. As the majority of you already know, she has knowledge and a skill set you can all learn from. So don't hesitate to take advantage of her being here with us today." Everyone applauded before Max threaded her arm through LJ's and led her to a small trailer she used for an office. "You can stow your things in here."

"Okay." LJ moved inside and could feel Max right behind her. For LJ, Max had been the ultimate fuck—primal, heart-pounding, hot sex. In the past, all Max needed to do was move close to her and LJ would become wet with arousal. It had been a long time since their last encounter, but the effect the woman had on her was still strong. Visions flooded LJ's head of nights of heated, unbridled passion while on digs that threatened to drive her over the edge. She found herself drawn to Max again and turned to face the woman.

"You know"—Max moved to within inches of LJ—"we should get together tonight and pick up where we left off." She let out a soft purr before leaning in and passionately kissing LJ.

LJ pushed her away, then stared into Max's darkened, lust-filled, hazel eyes. "Stop!" LJ scowled. "What the hell are you doing?"

Max grinned. "It's pretty obvious, unless I've lost my touch."

"This is not the time or the place. Try and remember where you are and who might be around before you pull something like that again," LJ growled. "I thought we had this same conversation on the dig in Peru."

"We did." In typical Max form, she laughed and then moved in to capture LJ's lips again. When LJ moved to avoid another kiss, Max took a step backward. "Are you playing hard to get, lover?" She gave LJ a once-over. "You kissed me back, and I can feel and smell your arousal. You'll come to me. You always do. Why else would you have come all the way out here?" She was looking directly at LJ's breasts, and she licked her lips before laughing again as she gazed at LJ's face. "Let's go out and get our hands dirty, and then later you can…" She winked. "…do anything you want to me."

"I didn't know you'd be here, so don't hold your breath." LJ brushed past the woman and escaped out the trailer's door. Inside she was trembling. Her body craved Max's touch and desired what only she could make it feel. LJ walked quickly away, trying to distance herself from the old feelings. In the background, she could still hear Max's familiar laughter.

The day passed quickly, and soon it was late afternoon. Helping the students made LJ feel refreshed and gave her a renewed sense of accomplishment. She waved at those around her and said, "Thanks, it was a great day," before going to the trailer to pick up her bag. Just as she was about to step back outside, Max came up to her.

"Well, looks like we're all done for today, lover." She moved in closer. "What do you say we get together tonight for some research for old times' sake?" She ran a finger along the ridge of LJ's breast. "I know how hungry you get after a day of digging in the dirt."

"I can't. I'm busy." LJ tried to move past her, but Max wouldn't budge.

Max squeezed a taut nipple. "I can tell you don't

mean that," she whispered. "Stop playing this hard-to-get game, because we both know what you want."

LJ closed her eyes, trying to squelch the fire raging inside her. Max was full of intense passion that could go on for hours. There was no commitment and no drama with Max. LJ made the mistake of looking into the smoldering, hazel eyes gazing at her with unbridled lust. It was her undoing.

"I'm not spending the night."

"I know. You never do, and I don't want you to."

LJ grabbed her hand. "Let's get out of here."

†

They had dinner at an out-of-the-way café. Max was her usual exuberant self and would often brush her fingers casually over LJ's cheek. Several times she rested her hand on LJ's thigh, slowly moving it in a back-and-forth motion. It was exhilarating.

When they arrived at Max's house, LJ looked around, noting that little had changed. Artifacts and mementoes of digs cluttered every available space. They didn't appear to be random though, but thoughtfully placed in groupings of similar objects.

Max came up behind her and wrapped her arms around LJ's waist. "I'd offer you a drink, but I'm pretty sure that isn't what either of us wants."

LJ turned in the embrace, and her lips hovered over Max's. "Is this what you had in mind?" She kissed her hard, demanding more.

"Bed now." Max grabbed her hand and dragged her to the bedroom, where she wasted no time in divesting LJ of her clothes. Her eyes raked over LJ's naked body, and she sucked in a breath. "Magnificent. Just as I remembered." She brushed her palms over erect nipples and smiled when they got harder.

LJ took her time undressing Max, teasing the bare skin with her lips as she revealed it. When Max had sex, she treated it like an archaeological dig. She'd explore everywhere, gently brushing away the layers, delving deeper and deeper until she discovered the prize. When she did, she'd take her time reveling in the discovery, kissing and touching before capturing what she was looking for and making it hers.

The quick fuck in a car with Cassie paled in comparison, and LJ knew at that moment that she'd never be with Cassie again. Max knew how to make her body hum, leaving her wanting more. Why hadn't she sought out Max instead of the singer? Max was like her—sex for sex's sake and nothing more. There were no entanglements or emotions, just a mind-blowing release.

†

The smell of coffee made LJ open her eyes. She looked around the room, realizing where she was before getting out of bed. After pulling on her t-shirt and going to the bathroom, she made her way to the kitchen, where a naked Max was leaning against the counter, drinking a cup of coffee.

"I thought you weren't spending the night." Max poured coffee into a mug and handed it to LJ.

"Want me to leave?" LJ grinned and took the offered cup. Her eyes raked over Max's body, and a sudden rush of desire filled her as she remembered their multiple couplings during the night.

"We need to be back to the site by ten. That's when everyone starts to arrive. I like to have coffee and donuts for them."

LJ looked at the time glowing red on the microwave, put down her coffee mug, stepped closer to Max, took her mug, placed it next to hers, and wrapped her arms around the woman. "That'll give us a couple of hours, then." She kissed Max hard before leading her back to the bedroom.

"I have a feeling we might be late," Max said as she swatted LJ's backside. "I can't think of a better way to spend an early Sunday morning. Do you remember how we'd celebrate a new day at that dig in Peru?"

LJ turned and put a finger over Max's lips. "Shut up and kiss me."

✝

Kylie fought the urge to join her parents and Ryan. The memory of LJ's lips on hers kept playing in her mind, and she found herself touching her lips and imagining she could still feel the softness. Instead, she'd spent the time deep-cleaning every closet, nook, and cranny, throwing out anything she deemed no longer needed. She also boxed up all Ted's things that she'd avoided doing anything with and took them to the Salvation Army. He wouldn't be back to claim any of them and she'd held on to them too long. It was time to move on, and that was exactly what she planned to do.

Late on Sunday afternoon, Kylie sat in the family room with her feet propped up on an ottoman. Although she'd worked herself to exhaustion, the memory of LJ's kiss still haunted her.

She heard the door open before Ryan came bursting into the room. Kylie had been moody and contemplative the entire weekend, but seeing Ryan righted her world, and she smiled for the first time since the encounter with LJ.

"How was your weekend?" Kylie held Ryan tightly in her arms. "I missed you."

"Granny loved seeing her." Virginia came up behind them and rubbed Kylie's back. "Dad has dinner."

"Did you stop at Ho Ho?" Kylie's eyes widened as her mouth watered in anticipation.

"Yes."

"We got fortune cookies too, Mommy."

Carl came through the front door laden with three plastic bags. "Delivery," he said, smiling. "We got all your favorites."

"And fortune cookies too," Ryan added.

Kylie laughed and got up to follow the others into the kitchen. "Do we need chopsticks?"

"Of course. What would takeout be without them?" Virginia began opening the containers. "Can you get some plates?"

Kylie opened a cupboard door and pulled out four plates before getting silverware and chopsticks out of a drawer. "This is perfect. I didn't realize how hungry I was until I smelled the kung pao chicken." She looked into the containers. "Oh, you got sushi too. Can this get any better?"

"Yes, it can. Granny sent you her chocolate bundt cake that you like so much."

"How is she doing?"

"You'd never know she is in her 'golden years.' She insisted on cooking for us, and she hasn't lost a beat in that department."

"She gave me this." Ryan fingered the heart necklace around her neck.

Kylie smiled. "She treasures that."

"Yes, she does," Virginia said. "She told me she always wanted Ryan to have it and thought she was old enough now to take care of it."

"I'll have to call her and thank her."

"She'd like to hear from you."

That evening after Ryan had a bath and Kylie tucked her in bed, she sat in a chair in the bedroom running her fingers over her lips. "How will I face her tomorrow?" She thought about quitting but nixed the idea immediately. She wanted to see LJ and be around her. The realization hit her that she wasn't going to deny herself any longer, even if it meant watching her from a distance. But in her heart, she knew saying that was easier than doing it.

Kylie looked at her watch and noted it was only eight o'clock. Certain her grandmother was still up, she picked up her cell phone, engaged FaceTime, and pressed in the number.

"Hi, Granny, thank you so much for the cake," Kylie said when she saw her. Looking at her granny, who at eighty-eight still insisted on sleeping with rollers in her hair, Kylie smiled.

"Kylie darling, it is so good to hear your voice. What a delight it was to see Ryan this weekend. The only thing missing was you."

"Sorry I wasn't there."

"What's wrong?"

"Nothing. I just wanted to see your face. I miss you."

"Kylie, I didn't spend all those days taking care of you when you were young not to know when you are troubled by something."

Kylie blew out a breath. Her mother was right. Granny was as sharp as she ever was. "I'm in a quandary, Granny."

"Thought so. What's got you so confused?"

"Why do you think I'm confused?"

"Kylie, I can see it in your face. You've got that line-between-your-eyes thing going on. Now out with it."

"I kissed someone and I can't stop thinking about it."

"Kissing is a good thing, and I highly recommend it. So why are you confused?"

Kylie sucked in a breath. She could see only love and kindness in her granny's face. "Because I kissed a woman."

Her Granny laughed. "Child, do you remember Rosie who lived with me after your grandfather died?"

"Yes. She always told me she was my other granny. What about her?"

Granny chuckled. "We did a lot of kissin'."

Kylie's eyes widened. "You and she were lovers?"

"Everyone, even your parents, thought she was my companion and nothing more—still do—but she was much more than that." She sighed, and sadness filled her eyes. "Rosie's been gone for a year now, and not a day goes by that I don't miss her."

"Oh, Granny, I remember how distraught you were when she passed." Kylie smiled at her granny and spread out her arms. "This is me giving you a big hug."

"Thank you. I want you to know you are not alone."

"What should I do? She doesn't want me."

"Does she know how you feel?"

"I kissed her."

"But did you tell her?"

"No."

"Child, Rosie and I danced around the issue for years until one day I told her that I loved her like a man loves a woman. I was amazed to find out that she had the same feelings for me."

"I wish it were that easy. This is complicated."

"Life is complicated, Kylie. If you don't take any chances, the best parts of it will pass you by."

"I know you're right, but still I don't know what to do."

"You'll know. I suspect you already do."

"Yes, I do. Thank you for talking to me and trusting me."

"I will be here for you as a sounding board whenever you need me, child."

"I know. Good night, Granny. I love you. Sweet dreams." Kylie blew a kiss, and her granny caught it just as she did every time they spoke.

"I love you too, my sweet girl. Good night."

Kylie watched as the image of her granny disappeared, and for the first time since kissing LJ, she felt a sense of peace.

Chapter Ten

At six a.m. as she did every weekday, LJ arrived at work on Monday. Max, along with the work in the field, had been just the tonic she needed. Her mind wandered back to the night she spent with Max. It had been exhilarating and terrifying at the same time, since every time she'd looked at Max, she'd seen Kylie. Now in a few hours she would have to face the woman whose kiss still lingered in her memory.

She'd had time at the dig on the weekend to bring things into perspective, and for the moment, her cool exterior was back in place. She resolved not to allow her emotions to rule her mind or body. She would conduct herself in a businesslike manner, starting with making no mention of the previous Friday night. She brushed her lips and closed her eyes. But how could she forget? Kissing Kylie was exactly what she'd wanted to do from the first moment she'd seen the woman.

"Forget it. You aren't doing yourself or her any favors by dwelling on what happened. It's over and done with."

With her coffee in hand, she entered the workroom, looking for other clues that might lead to what the curious glyph meant. Finding the piece that Kylie was working on last Friday, LJ put on her gloves and inspected it. She immediately recognized why Kylie had had a problem. Then she began picking up various photos and scrutinized them, trying to find something that looked similar to the glyph or to the fragments she was putting together.

Over the weekend with the students and volunteers, LJ realized she hadn't taken enough time to teach Kylie about the purpose behind the work she was doing. Sure, on occasions she would talk to her about the Wari' or give her suggestions on improving her work, but she hadn't done any real mentoring. Kylie had taken a few undergraduate courses, but years had passed since she'd actually had any hands-on experience. LJ resolved to act like the educator she had been trained to be and began studying the artifacts to see what she could teach Kylie about them.

A thought forced its way past her defenses, and she shivered. *What if Kylie quits?* LJ couldn't believe how devastated the idea made her feel. Not paying attention to anything but the piece in front of her, she swallowed hard and tried not to focus on the panic that filled her mind.

†

Standing at the door to the museum, Kylie debated whether to go inside or not. Just thinking about her actions on Friday night made her blush. The feel of LJ's kiss was still fresh in her mind. *So soft...stop it!* How could she ever face LJ again? *What a fool I was.* She sighed deeply.

Her granny's words ricocheted in her mind, and she knew she had two choices—quit or stay. In her heart, she knew if she quit now, she'd spend the rest of her life regretting the action. This was her brass ring, and thanks to her granny's advice, she knew reaching out and grabbing it was her only option. After sucking in a breath, Kylie opened the door.

Once inside, she quickly hung up her jacket in her locker and went to the workroom, where she had been piecing together what looked like a plate. If she kept a low profile, maybe LJ wouldn't see her or her embarrassment. No such luck. LJ was standing at her worktable. *Shit, can this day get any better?* She coughed slightly and flushed in embarrassment as LJ turned in her direction.

"Good morning. I...I didn't expect to see you in here this early. You usually don't come in here until lunchtime." Kylie avoided looking at LJ as she went straight to her current project. She began working immediately, desperately trying to ignore the woman's presence or her gaze.

LJ moved to where she was sitting. "Is this the piece you had trouble with on Friday?" she asked softly.

"Yes, it seems to be missing some parts." Kylie still avoided looking at her blue eyes. It would be her undoing.

LJ picked up a pencil and started to sketch something on a pad of paper on the table. "It's supposed to look something like this. You have to look beyond what you think you see to what is. It is kind of like looking outside the box. If you haven't any preconceived ideas of what it is and just look at the parts for what they are—parts—then you may have an easier time of it. From what I can see, there isn't enough here to make a complete piece. It looks to be some sort of plate or tray. Why don't you try to form something that resembles this and then see what you need? It is not often that we can find all the pieces like you did on some of the other artifacts."

LJ was too close to her. The bitter disappointment and embarrassment of Friday was still fresh in Kylie's mind. *I won't be doing that again anytime soon.* "I see. I will try that. Thank you." She kept her head down, refusing to look directly at LJ.

LJ put the fragile fragments down and moved to another area. "When you are done with that, I want you to look over here and see what you can do."

Kylie could feel LJ's eyes on her and nodded in acknowledgement. "Okay, I'll do that. Anything else?"

"No." LJ started for the door. "Keep up the good work."

"Thank you." Only when she heard LJ's footsteps fading did Kylie look up to see the back of the woman disappear out the doorway. *What just happened? She was acting as though Friday never happened.* Kylie shrugged and raised her eyebrows. "So was I," she murmured. Kylie closed her eyes and took a deep breath, trying to get a handle on the recent occurrence. "If I try to figure it out it will drive me mad." With a shake of her head, she looked at the artifact, and it wasn't long before she became lost trying to visualize the object LJ had described.

When LJ returned with lunch at noon, Kylie's stomach roiled, and it had nothing to do with being hungry.

"How's it going?" LJ put the lunch bag on the now-customary stool.

"I did what you suggested, and it is taking shape." Kylie lifted the object.

LJ gave her a rare smile, then took a step closer to her, and Kylie closed her eyes, relishing in the pleasure the simple move gave her.

"Well done. It all has to do with perspective and expectations."

"I can see that now." Kylie wondered if LJ knew she made an analogy for the events of Friday night or if it was a coincidence. "Would you like to share the turkey wrap with me?"

LJ moved around the table and pointed to one of the artifacts. "Remember that I want you to work on this one next."

Kylie nodded and looked away. "I remember." As hard as she tried, she couldn't keep the disappointment out of her voice at LJ's non-answer.

Kylie then realized LJ might be just as uncomfortable as she was about the kiss. *This is her way of distancing herself from the incident and me.* Whether or not LJ was really doing that, Kylie could live with that plan. She too needed to feel a sense of detachment regarding LJ, just as she suspected LJ needed to feel that from her. Or so she thought until she touched her lips.

"Okay. Keep up the good work."

After LJ left the room, Kylie let out the breath she'd been holding and began to tremble. Being that close to LJ made her feel things she wasn't ready to acknowledge. Or had she? Wasn't that what she and her granny had spoken about? "Maybe I should talk to Granny again."

†

The next month was intense for LJ. Kylie restored more pieces of pottery on which the unknown glyph appeared partially and sometimes fully. The number of pieces intensified LJ's need to discover the glyph's meaning, which required her to spend the morning mentoring and working alongside Kylie in the resurrection of the artifacts.

"Maybe you should hire a few more people," Kylie

said.

"I wouldn't have to hire anyone. I can always get some graduate students from the university to come in several days a week." She shook her head. "But what we are doing is far too important to trust the restorations with them. You are the only one I feel comfortable with doing this job."

Kylie blushed, and LJ thought it was cute. Kylie motioned to the multitude of artifact pieces waiting for attention. "Surely others can work on some of these. Otherwise it will take years."

LJ put down what she was doing. "You're forgetting one of the basic tenets of archaeology—patience." She fixed Kylie with an intense gaze, and not for the first time warmth spread throughout her body. "We will get there."

"Not if all of them are as difficult as the one I'm working on now."

LJ got up and went around the table to stand next to Kylie. When she leaned in to look at what she was doing, the closeness overwhelmed her. A month earlier, she would have denied her feelings by turning and running away. Now, just being that close to Kylie was exhilarating. It was a feeling that she could not deny or give up.

"Let's see what you've got."

"Do you see this part here with the rounded edge and the indentation?"

"Yes." LJ inhaled the fresh, clean scent she now associated with Kylie. She couldn't identify what it was, but it was intoxicating.

"It makes no sense. Even if I try to envision this as something other than what it looks like—a plate—I see no place that it belongs."

LJ rested her hand on Kylie's shoulder as she leaned in to take a closer look through the magnifying glass. When

Kylie trembled beneath her touch, she removed her hand. "This is a prime example of why I don't want anyone else working here. It does not belong to this piece. Some idiot wasn't meticulous. That's what happens when I let...." She waved her hand, realizing what she was about to say about unqualified people could also apply to Kylie's technical lack of qualifications "I loathe incompetence."

"Perhaps all that's needed is a great teacher. I'm so fortunate you took a chance on me, gave me this job and taught me so much over the last months."

LJ took a step back, needing to remove herself from the tender feelings that were demanding attention. *So much for distancing myself from her.* "You're doing a great job, Kylie. At times I think *I* am the fortunate one."

Kylie immediately felt bereft when LJ moved away. Her attraction to LJ had rapidly increased after LJ began spending her mornings in the workroom. LJ did nothing to give away her feelings about the situation though. On many occasions, it was as if she wanted to say something but would immediately school her features. Kylie wished she could read LJ's mind and know what she was feeling.

Kylie had spoken with her granny three times, trying to figure out all the emotions being around LJ was evoking in her. She recalled the conversation they had the night before on FaceTime.

"Granny, I don't know what to do."

"Why, child? It seems to me it should be pretty straightforward."

"That's just it...it isn't. Yes, we kissed, but we dance

around it like it never happened."

"So why haven't you told her how you feel?"

"Oh, I couldn't do that. What if she tells me to get lost or fires me?"

Her granny shook her head and smiled. "Do you really think that will happen?"

"I don't know."

"You know I went through the same debate with myself when I was trying to figure out how to tell Rosie. I was certain she'd go running for the hills. She didn't."

"But LJ isn't Rosie." Kylie shrugged. "There are times when I just want to shake her and say, 'Look at me.' Other times I hide from her, afraid she'll see my true feelings."

Her granny smiled. "You never have been one to hide how you feel. Don't you think she knows?"

Kylie laughed. "If she does, then I can only come to one conclusion...she's not interested."

"Does that mean you should give up?"

"No. Not at all. I just have to get it all figured out, that's all."

"If you do what your heart tells you, then you can't go wrong."

"Even if she walks away?"

"Is that what your heart is telling you?"

"No."

"Then listen to your heart, child, and trust in what it says."

As usual her granny was right. She needed to devise a plan to get LJ to socialize with her, at least. When LJ touched her shoulder, Kylie's whole body tingled with pleasure, making her want to lean in and ask for more. The time they were spending together was becoming comfortable, and she didn't want to upset that feeling with unwanted advances. She'd settle for dreaming and fantasizing about LJ in those private moments before falling asleep.

She looked at LJ, who seemed focused on the dilemma of sorting through of pieces. "LJ, would you like to come for dinner tonight? We're having lasagna."

LJ looked up. "Sounds fantastic, but I have to pass. The only time I can speak to my colleagues around the world about this glyph is in the evening or early morning."

"Maybe just for one night you can relax." Kylie smiled. "Aren't you the one who tells me to take a step back and return with new eyes?"

A deep, rich laugh filled the room. "That I do, but tonight I'm speaking with Yuri Andropov, who I've been playing phone tag with for a week."

Kylie tried to hide her disappointment and smiled. "Maybe if you can't do dinner, we could go out for a drink and discuss the next steps in solving the mystery."

LJ gave her a perplexed look. "I don't think so."

"God, I sound pathetic," she mumbled.

"What was that?"

Kylie shook her head, shocked that she'd actually said that out loud. "Nothing." She bit on her lip as LJ nodded before returning to what she'd been doing.

†

Weeks passed, and LJ worked long into the nights, pouring over volume after volume, trying to decipher the meaning of the find. She'd contacted overseas colleagues and discussed the photos she'd sent them, hoping they might be able to shed some light on the puzzle. Often she would stay until midnight before going home to shower and sleep for a few hours before arriving back in her office four in the morning.

She was exhausted. Her brain was beginning to shut down from all the data she was trying to comprehend. Holly's voice echoed in her ears telling her to "Walk away from the problem." She smiled as she recalled how her lover always seemed to be able to make the most complicated situation simple.

LJ closed her eyes, and her mind drifted back to happier times when life didn't demand so much of her. *To be there again* was her whimsical thought before a familiar voice brought her back to reality.

"Good morning. Hey, are you okay?"

She turned and actually smiled. It was as if Kylie had been reading her mind. "It's nothing a week's sleep won't cure." LJ closed her eyes and stretched her body exaggeratedly, suddenly realizing exactly how tired it and her mind were.

"Why don't you give yourself permission to take a night off and come home with me and have a good home-cooked meal? Bet it's been a while since you had one of those."

Leaning back in her chair, LJ sighed before closing her eyes once again in disbelief. The woman, whom she had been rude, nasty, and cold toward, only ever spoke to her with kindness and compassion. It was time for her to reciprocate. "I would like that very much. Thank you." After swiveling around in her chair, she looked straight at Kylie. "Want me to bring anything?"

Her reward for her question was a goofy grin. "Nope. You aren't a picky eater, are you?" Kylie's tone was playful.

LJ smirked at the notion. "I've sat in the jungle and eaten bugs, so I don't think there's anything you could serve that I won't eat."

"Good, is six okay with you?"

"I'll be there." LJ turned back to her desk and the volumes waiting for her before she added, "Um, Kylie, will I need a map to get there?"

Kylie laughed. "Hey, you've hacked your way through dense jungle undergrowth. I bet you can find your way to my home."

LJ could hear her laughing all the way to the workroom. She looked at the space that just moments before had held the blonde. How could Kylie be nice to her after the horrible way she'd treated her? *No one ever cared about me like that, except....*

†

With each day that passed, Kylie couldn't help but notice how haggard LJ was looking. Every time LJ came into the workroom, the dark circles around her eyes seemed to grow more pronounced. LJ had finally accepted a dinner invitation, and Kylie's mind began to whirl over what to make. She'd have to stop by the market after picking up Ryan from school and buy some fresh vegetables. *I bet she doesn't eat many of those.*

She knew LJ's penchant for getting involved in what she was doing and forgetting the time and wasn't foolish enough to think LJ would actually show up. That thought stabbed at her heart. But on the off chance that she did, Kylie would have a decent meal prepared.

Back in the workroom, she mulled over the last few months, during which they'd developed a companionable routine of working together. Yet the kiss they'd shared that night at the Rusty Nail was always in the forefront of Kylie's mind. She often wondered if LJ thought about it too.

Kylie's attraction grew every time she was near LJ. Her mind once again focused, as it had many times, on the day Maxine Dylan came breezing into the workroom with her arm entwined in LJ's.

"Well hello there." The woman's voice was low and smoky. She was smiling.

"Kylie, this is Dr. Maxine Dylan. She's dean of the anthropology department at the university." LJ turned to the woman. "Max, this is my assistant, Kylie Wilcox."

Kylie took the offered hand and shook it with her eyes fixed on the possessive way the woman held on to LJ's arm. "Nice to meet you, Dr. Dylan."

"You can call me Max." She turned to LJ and said in a loud whisper, "You didn't tell me you had such a hottie working for you."

Heat rose to Kylie's cheeks. The way Max was hanging on LJ sent a wave of jealousy through her. She involuntarily ran her fingers through her hair, feeling uncomfortable and wishing they would leave. From the look on LJ's face, Kylie suspected that she too was embarrassed. "Is there something you need me to do?"

Pulling her arm free, LJ shook her head. "No. Max was on the dig and wanted to see the progress we're making."

"We had a spectacular time digging and not digging." Max lifted her eyebrows and winked. "Didn't we, darling?" She trailed a finger down LJ's arm.

Kylie wanted to rip the woman's hand off. *At least*

this one is a step up from that skanky singer. Her heart sank. Clearly Max and LJ had a history "Well, I'll get back to work, then." Kylie turned back to the table, refusing to let either woman see the tears of disappointment stinging the backs of her eyes.

"Let's go to your office and lock the door. I want to have my way with you," Max whispered loud enough for Kylie to hear.

"No. Not today. I have work to do."

Max laughed. "You're far too tense to do any work just yet. You need to relax, and I know just how to get you there."

LJ sighed before Kylie heard them walking away.

†

The market was crowded, and the checkout lines were long. *Why is it that every time I'm in a hurry, there's a lack of cashiers?* She stood clutching the basket and listening to Ryan chatter about her day at school while mentally preparing the meal she hoped LJ would like.

Once home, Kylie scurried around the kitchen making a quick and easy, last minute dinner of four ingredients—baked pesto chicken, couscous, fresh green beans, and a salad. Kylie looked at what she'd created, noting that it only needed finishing touches before glancing at the clock on the stove. It was inching toward six o'clock, and she wondered again if LJ would show up. If she didn't, she'd have leftovers that would be good the next day. Disappointment surged through her when the red numbers on the microwave turned to 6:05.

"Mommy, when are we going to eat?" Ryan asked. "I'm starving."

"I doubt you are starving, and we'll eat in a little bit, baby. I'm waiting for a friend to arrive to have dinner with us."

"Who?"

Kylie smiled. "A woman I work with. Now go wash your hands. Everything is ready, so we can eat as soon as she gets here."

"Okay, but I really am starving."

✝

LJ went to her small apartment to take a shower before going to Kylie's home for dinner. She'd gotten Kylie's address from her employment application and punched it into the GPS app on her phone. On her way there, she considered stopping for wine but decided against it. In her current state, one glass and she would be a goner and she still had a long night of phone calls planned. After pulling her truck into the driveway, she looked at the house. Although the brick Garrison colonial looked big, it appeared welcoming. She paused, trying to convince herself that accepting the invitation was craziness and she should leave while she still could. *I don't want to leave.* She wanted to go into the warm home and, for a brief moment, hoped she'd find some sort of peace.

LJ sucked in a deep breath, got out of the truck, and headed for the door. Happiness filled her for the first time in longer than she could remember as she pressed the doorbell. A small voice behind it said, "I'll get it, Mommy," before the door swung open. To her surprise, a miniature version of Kylie stood behind it. "Hi, my name is, Ryan. Who are you?" she asked.

Not able to help herself, LJ smiled broadly before

squatting to the child's level and holding out her hand. "Hi, Ryan, my name is LJ." She lifted her head and saw Kylie standing behind her daughter, looking more beautiful than she had ever seen her. LJ's heart did a flip and her stomach filled with knots. *My God, she's stunning.*

Kylie smiled. "Hi, glad you could make it. I see you have already met my daughter. Ryan, did you introduce yourself?"

"Yes, Mommy."

A smile crossed Kylie's face. "Come on in, dinner is almost ready. Are you hungry?"

LJ moved inside, and Ryan quickly grabbed her hand. "Want to come see my Barbie doll?"

Fear coursed through LJ. Of all the dangers she had faced in her life, nothing for some reason she didn't understand, the thought of talking to this child scared her. "Hmm, why don't I help your mom first, then we can take a look."

"Ryan, did you wash your hands like I told you to?" Kylie gently touched her daughter's shoulder and gave her an I-mean-business look.

"Yes, Mommy. Can I go get my doll now?"

"After dinner you can bring your doll down to show our guest."

Ryan pulled a face. "Okay, Mommy."

"Sorry about that. She usually doesn't let just anyone play with her Barbie. I think she must like you. Do you want anything to drink?" Kylie gave her a thin smile. "Come on in and have a seat. Dinner will be ready as soon as I put it on the table." Her face reddened. "Sorry, I seem to be babbling." She shrugged. "Guess I'm nervous. You're the first person I've had for dinner since Ted died."

LJ's eyes widened, and she took a deep breath to

calm the anxiety that was bubbling up. The last thing she wanted to do was discuss anything personal with Kylie, and her dead husband was about as personal as it got. Unless, of course, they discussed the kiss that hung between them like an icy curtain of denial. She pursed her lips and took a deep breath. "Would you like some help?"

"Sure. Come on, I can always use help."

Mostly LJ just stood observing Kylie maneuver around the kitchen as she put the final touches on the meal. As she surreptitiously watched the woman, the warm, tender feelings she had been squelching for many months screamed to come alive.

"Can you put these bowls on the table?"

Lost in her thoughts, LJ didn't response.

"LJ, will you please put these on the table?" Kylie held two bowls out to her.

"Sure." As she took them, a chill of excitement ran through body when their fingers brushed.

The food was wonderful. LJ couldn't remember when she'd last had a decent meal. She listened to Ryan's endless chatter and was surprised when she found it rather amusing instead of irritating. From time to time, she would glance in Kylie's direction and was pleased when Kylie looked back at her.

"Kylie, thank you. That was excellent. I can't recall when I've had a better meal." She knew her smile was as genuine as her words. For a long moment, she stared at Kylie until Ryan jumped out of her chair and grabbed her hand.

"Come on," the young girl squealed. "My Barbie is in my room.

"Ryan, I don't think LJ wants—"

"It's okay. I don't mind." LJ winked at Kylie, then headed up the stairs, wondering what the hell she was getting herself into.

Little kids and puppies always thaw the coldest of hearts. Kylie stood shaking her head as she watched Ryan lead LJ out of the room. "I do believe behind that icy exterior is a heart of mush. Wonders never cease," she whispered while clearing the table. As the meal had progressed, she'd noticed that LJ began to relax and the tired tension that had seeped onto her face lately began to disappear. Her stomach summersaulted whenever LJ laughed, and a contented smile curved her lips. *Maybe once I get Ryan in bed we can sit and talk. I'd like that.*

She hurried to put the dishes into the dishwasher, desperate to go upstairs and watch as LJ and Ryan played with Barbie. Knowing she'd look too obvious and intrusive, she nixed the idea. Yet, the attraction and need remained, and she walked toward the staircase only to stop and go back to what she was doing in the kitchen. LJ had made it perfectly clear she had no interest in her, and Kylie had no choice but to go along with that. *For now.*

✝

Barbie, LJ found out, was a skinny, busty, blonde clothes hog who always stood on her toes. An animated Ryan put on a fashion show of the latest Barbie fashions, and LJ watched, amazed by the young girl's creativity and joy. She surprised herself by actually laughing a few times.

"Ryan, what do you say we go down and keep your mom company?" she finally asked.

The child's face lit up. "Mommy needs me to be with her. She likes hugging me, and sometimes Mommy gets lonely and cries. Will you carry me?"

"Sure I will." Completely out of character, LJ picked Ryan up and carried her down the stairs. All the while, her head was spinning with the disturbing feelings the thought of Kylie crying brought to her.

✝

Sitting in the living room, Kylie could hear Ryan's laughter and LJ's low tones. They had been upstairs for twenty minutes, and she had been debating again whether it would be wise to go up and see what was happening when they came down the stairs. Her eyes widened when she saw Ryan in LJ's arms.

"Looks like you two had a good time with Barbie," she said.

"Mommy, Lgie is a really good Barbie player."

"Her name is LJ, and did she tell you to call her that?"

"I did," LJ said.

"Okay, but you have to say LJ, not Lgie."

"It's okay, Kylie. I've never had a nickname before."

Kylie gave LJ a skeptical look. "Are you sure?" Her eyes lingered on LJ a moment too long, and she quickly looked away.

"Yes."

"Mommy, can Lgie come back and play with me again?"

"We'll see, Pumpkin." Kylie bent down and gave her daughter a hug and a kiss. "Now, why don't you get ready for bed, then I will tuck you in."

"But Mommy…."

"No buts, Ryan, you know the rules. Now go and get

ready for bed."

"Okay." Ryan pulled a pathetic face and started back up the stairs but stopped, turned around, and looked at LJ with a pitiful expression. "Will you tuck me in too, Lgie?"

"Sure I will."

"You don't have to do that." Kylie gave LJ and apologetic look. "She gets carried away at times, especially when she really likes someone."

"I have no experience where kids are concerned, but I find your daughter very entertaining." LJ smiled. "Can't say I've ever tucked someone in, so I'm not sure what that entails, but I'll give it a try."

"Just follow my lead."

†

After Kylie and LJ tucked Ryan in, a calm quiet filled the house.

"I made a pot of coffee. Would you like a cup?"

LJ rubbed her hand over her face. "Yeah, that would be nice." She was exhausted but didn't want the night to end, and the coffee would keep her engine running.

Kylie's face seemed to glow with happiness. "Great. Why don't you go in the living room and I'll be right in?"

LJ lowered her weary body onto the soft leather couch and sighed. The evening with Kylie and her daughter had proven to be more enjoyable than she'd ever expected. *I should have accepted an offer for dinner sooner. Don't know what I was afraid of.* But when Kylie entered the room, she knew instantly what had scared her. She started to rise. "Let me help you."

"No need. I have it." Kylie placed the tray with the mugs on the coffee table. "I brought some cookies too. Ryan

125

and I made them."

LJ uncharacteristically patted the seat next to her. "Come on and sit down. The meal and the night were wonderful. Thank you for asking me." She smiled and let out a contented sigh. "It was exactly what I needed."

"You know you're welcome to come for dinner anytime you want."

"I wouldn't want to impose."

"You wouldn't…ever." Kylie picked up the plate of cookies. "Would you like one?"

"Mmm-hmm, they look delicious." LJ couldn't believe how easy it was to carry on a non-work conversation with Kylie. Just sitting so close made her heart beat double time and her body smolder. There was absolutely no doubt in her mind that she wanted more from Kylie than just a meal.

"If you like them I'll send you home with some." Kylie laughed. "I don't know what I was thinking when we made them. There's only the two of us, and I made enough for an army."

LJ bit into the rich, buttery cookie, and it melted in her mouth. "These are delicious. I don't think I've ever had a better one."

Kylie smiled. "Then I will definitely give you some to take home." She reached for her cup at the same time LJ reached for hers, and their hands touched. That was all it took as their eyes met, then their lips. Explosions of all kinds were going off inside of Kylie. There was no doubt that she wanted LJ in ways she'd never imagined herself wanting a woman. For months now, she had fantasized about this very moment, and now that it was coming true, she could feel her body collapsing at the power it created. As the kiss intensified, she lost herself in emotions and needs that were foreign but strangely familiar.

It was clear to Kylie that LJ too was also lost in their kisses. Being in her arms felt so wonderful, and she desperately needed to feel closer. She wanted this more than she'd ever wanted anything else. "Make love to me. Please," she begged.

LJ began to move her hands over Kylie's trembling body, and Kylie moaned with delight, deepening the kiss with her tongue.

LJ suddenly pulled away. "I can't," her muffled, intense voice said.

"Yes. Yes, you can. It's what we both want." Kylie moved in to capture LJ's lips again. She wasn't going to let LJ get away. Not this time.

LJ moved and then stood. "I can't. I just can't."

"But you can with that singer and Dr. Dylan. What's wrong with me? If it's because I work for you, I'll quit." Kylie's body was on fire, and she looked up at LJ in confusion. There was no way she'd misread the desire and need in the kisses they'd shared.

"You don't understand, that singer meant nothing to me."

"And Dr. Dylan, is she nothing too?"

LJ waved a hand. "She's someone I use for casual sex, and that's all." She caressed Kylie's face. "You deserve better than a convenient fuck." She shook her head. "Don't you see? That's all I can offer you. I can't give you more than that."

LJ's eyes were still dark with desire. "That isn't good enough. Why, LJ? What's wrong with me?"

"Kylie, there's nothing wrong with you. You're perfect. You are asking me to climb to the top of Kukulcan's

Temple and I am telling you I don't have any feet, but you still want me to climb the three hundred and sixty-five steps. I just can't. Don't you get that?"

Kylie began to sob. "All that I get is that you don't want me."

LJ moved closer and sat back down next to Kylie before taking her hands and gazing at her. "Kylie, you are not a one-night stand. You're forever, and I just can't give you that right now. I might never be able to." She pulled Kylie close and held her tight. "I need time," she whispered.

Kylie sank into the strong arms and sobbed. She understood what LJ was saying but was unable to accept it as final. Tomorrow was another day, and she'd find a way. She yawned and closed her eyes. "Please don't leave me."

"I'll stay until you're settled. Close your eyes. I've got you." LJ held Kylie for a long time while she drifted off to sleep, wondering what she was going to do. Her mind and body wanted Kylie—had always wanted her—but giving in to that meant committing totally to her. If she did that, she'd have to let go of the past. Could she do that? Holly was her lifeline. She was something familiar that was always there when LJ was down or needed comfort. The idea of abandoning Holly's memory for the unknown terrified her. There was every possibility that she would be nothing more than a curiosity for the straight woman in her arms. LJ lifted an eyebrow, grinning despite the situation. *She certainly didn't kiss me like she was only curious.*

LJ carefully disengaged herself from the sleeping woman and laid her down on the sofa before placing a woolen blanket from the back of the couch over her. She took the coffee cups to the kitchen, where she rinsed them and put them in the dishwasher. Then she made sure that all the doors were secure. Next, she went upstairs to check on Ryan. The girl had kicked her covers off, and LJ gently pulled the blankets back over her. She then bent down and placed a soft kiss on Ryan's cheek. "Sleep well, little one," she whispered as she left the room.

Back downstairs, she stood beside the couch and watched Kylie sleeping. "I wish I could give you what you want." She bent down and kissed her lightly on the lips, Kylie moaned softly, and her lips turned into what looked like a slight smile. For a moment longer, she stood gazing down on Kylie before sighing and starting for the door with a heavy heart. She engaged the lock and left the house.

In her truck, LJ hesitated before putting the key in the ignition. It would be so easy for her to stay and explore the possibilities Kylie was offering. *Why am I so afraid?* "Because I never felt this connected with Holly, and that scares me." Astounded by that realization, LJ knew she couldn't risk giving her heart away only to have it broken all over again.

LJ returned to the museum and made several calls to colleagues in Australia and New Zealand. They were as baffled as she was about the winged figure. She checked the names off her list and yawned. She'd return to her apartment and sleep for a few hours before coming back to try reach several prominent archaeologists in London.

After returning to her apartment, LJ looked around and noticed perhaps for the first time just how devoid of life it was. She stripped, crawled into bed, and fell asleep immediately, letting the physical, mental, and emotional exhaustion finally claim her.

129

Sometime in the middle of the night, Kylie woke with a start. "Why am I on the couch?" She gently touched her lips as she recalled how wonderful LJ's kisses felt. After folding the blanket and going to her bedroom, she stripped and crawled into her large, lonely bed. The next thing she knew, her alarm was going off and it was time to face the day.

Chapter Eleven

Sleep eluded her. LJ may have managed a minute or two but nothing more. All her thoughts were of Kylie and the moments they'd shared kissing on her couch. She knew without a doubt that if she hadn't had stopped, she would have taken Kylie to bed and made love with her. That would have been the biggest mistake of her life. There was no way she would let another love affair suck her in and break her heart. They were far too perilous, and there was no way she'd risk the heartache again. *No matter how good she makes me feel.*

The clock by her bed said it was three in the morning, and she was exhausted, but she had to make those phone calls, so she couldn't risk going back to sleep. She also needed to devise a plan that would let her teach Kylie without having contact of any sort with her. That meant no more sharing lunch or mornings in the workroom. The thought stabbed at her heart, but she didn't trust herself to be around Kylie and not take her in her arms. Sadness engulfed her. She'd looked forward to working with Kylie every morning, and not having that would be almost too much to bear. However, she'd shoulder the disappointment because she knew not doing so would bring about her demise.

Just as the clock rounded its hands to point to the three and six, she was dressed and had a plan in place that would allow her to avoid Kylie while mentoring her. It was simple. She'd leave Kylie instructions and have her lunch delivered directly to her.

It was cruel and she knew that Kylie deserved better. However, LJ's worn-out body and mind didn't have the strength to fight her attraction if she was around Kylie for even the minutes it took to deliver lunch. By avoiding her, she wouldn't have to see the hurt in her trusting, warm, gray eyes or the defeated slump of her shoulders. She was using Holly as a shield to keep Kylie at a distance, but her determination was waning. If she let that happen, it would be her undoing, and she resolved to be strong and avoid temptation at all costs. She had no doubt that she'd come to regret her actions, but she'd soldier on nonetheless.

"I'm a bitch," she muttered as she made her way to her truck. When she turned the key to start the engine, she thought for a moment that she should surrender to her emotions. With a quick shake of her head, she put the gear in drive and her foot to the gas pedal and took off. No way would she let herself fall into a relationship with Kylie, particularly after meeting Ryan. The young girl needed stability, and she couldn't give her that.

†

At some point over the last month and a half, Kylie's fantasies about LJ had turned from brief encounters at work to a hot, lusty romance. A search online resulted in a bevy of lesbian romances and movies, and she eagerly download several. She was surprised at how turned on she was when she watched or read the love scenes in them. She had never thought of other women that way, but she wasn't shocked or disgusted by her reaction. It seemed perfectly natural to her, and if she were honest with herself, she'd always found women attractive. She'd just never considered having sex with them and wondered why not.

While she drove to work, Kylie's mind was a jumble of confusing thoughts regarding LJ and her job. How was she going to face her after she'd practically thrown herself at the woman the previous night? With trepidation she opened the door to the museum and went down the stairs and toward the workroom. She frowned at the closed door to the catacombs and LJ's office. In the months she had worked there, she could never recall not having access to that area. She shrugged, figuring LJ was just as uncomfortable as she was and continued on to her locker, where she stored her belongings along with a tin of cookies she'd brought for LJ.

In the workroom, she saw several Post-its attached near different pieces she had been working on. That wasn't unusual since LJ often left similar notes regarding the reconstruction of some of the objects. She began working her way through them.

K,
You will need to rework this piece. Note that the right side is not fitting correctly. I think you should remember what I said about trying to visualize the whole piece and realizing it may not all be there.
LJ

K,

Note that the glyph is prominent on this piece, so be careful with it for it might hold the clue to what it means.
LJ

K,

This is good work. Go to section 15A next.
LJ

Something was different in the tone of these notes, and she wasn't sure what that was. Red flags were flying and slapping her in the face, insisting that she take notice. She had no doubt that LJ's absence had everything to do with the night before. With a heavy heart and trembling lips, she put the notes back where she had found them and began working.

"I had my chance and I blew it." She wouldn't give in to the tears that stung her eyes and threatened to fall. LJ would come around, and Kylie would wait for as long as that took because she refused to give up. She snickered at the absurdity of the situation. For the first time in her life, she'd gone headlong into something without thinking and it was backfiring on her. How would LJ know she was serious? *I was married and have a child, for God's sake. That certainly doesn't scream "I want to be have a relationship with you."*

As the morning passed, Kylie became so lost in her work that she didn't notice the time until her stomach began to rumble. When she looked at the clock and saw it was past noon, the sudden realization that LJ wasn't bringing her lunch devastated her in a way she'd never imagined anything could...except if something happened to someone in her immediate family. Still, she held her tears in check. Ted's death hadn't made her feel as distressed or heartbroken as she did at that moment. Then her heart rate picked up a beat as she heard footsteps coming into the room, but they sounded wrong. *Maybe she lost track of time.* When she looked up, a young girl came into sight holding a familiar bag that she knew contained her lunch.

"You Wilcox?" the girl gruffly asked.

"Yes, who are you?" Kylie, feeling her insides tremble, knew who the girl was.

"Got a delivery for you. It's tuna on whole wheat and a kale-and-spinach side salad with balsamic vinaigrette." She handed Kylie the bag and stood there waiting.

"I didn't order that," Kylie informed her.

"Sure you did." The girl looked at the receipt. "And it's been paid for." A quizzical expression came across her face. "You are K. Wilcox, aren't you?"

Kylie's heart was crying as she realized what was happening. "Yes, I'm K. Wilcox," she said dejectedly. She pulled a bill out of her pocket and handed it to the girl.

"Thank you, ma'am, but the tip was already paid for."

"Keep it anyway." Kylie took the bag and placed it on a nearby stool. "Thank you," she whispered as the girl left the room.

Was this how it was going to be from now on? Would their only contact be through notes and a delivery girl? Kylie looked at the bag with a sinking heart. She was no longer hungry, and the sooner she got her work done, the faster she could leave.

"I ruined everything," she sobbed. The tears that had threatened all morning finally brimmed in her eyes before rolling down her cheeks. "Damn, what am I going to do?" She sucked in a breath. "I'll call Granny. She'll know."

†

LJ's heart was hammering as she heard Kylie's footsteps going down the hall at the end of the day. She had spent the alone hours checking the references for her academic paper about the Wari' tribe but her mind kept drifting to Kylie. What she had to do was ignore the ache in her chest and distance herself from Kylie. To LJ that meant complete isolation if she was going to survive with her heart intact.

Survive to be alone. Are you sure that's what you want? It wasn't what she wanted, but she had to do this to stay alive. She had the sudden realization that Kylie would be a reason to want to stay alive, but she ignored it.

LJ had lingered in the corridor after the delivery, knowing she was responsible for Kylie softly crying. The sound almost broke LJ's resolve not to go to Kylie and give her an explanation. The vibration of her cell phone stopped her. When she saw the number of a French colleague on the screen, she was grateful. In the end, she knew this was best for them both, even though her heart was screaming a different message.

After waiting another half hour after Kylie left, LJ opened her door and found a cookie tin sitting on the floor outside. She picked it up before gently stroking the lid.

"She said she'd give me cookies. Must have brought them in this morning, and her reward was a shut door and a cold shoulder." LJ shook her head. "What an ass I am."

She strode down the corridor to the workroom. Her heart dropped when she noticed the unopened lunch bag resting on the stool. Kylie hadn't eaten, and that knowledge stabbed at LJ's heart. In the work area, she noted Kylie had finished everything she was working on and had started several new pieces. LJ shook her head and sighed. She sat and began piecing together what looked like a vase of some sort. Several hours later, she wrote a few notes for Kylie, then picked up the lunch bag. Her mind floated back to a time when she and Holly were first becoming friends and how they had pledged to be friends for life.

She suddenly realized that after Holly, she'd never had a friend again. No one. Zilch. Nada. The reality of that hit her between the eyes. Kylie had offered her friendship from day one, and she'd thrown it away. For what? Fear?

"What do you want the outcome to be when people or events puzzle you?" was a question Holly often asked her. If she were honest, she'd say she wanted Kylie in her life. However, there was a big stumbling block—she was afraid of losing someone again. "I just can't take that chance."

She looked around the workroom, visualizing Kylie there and sighed. "It can never be."

LJ left the museum long after sunset and drove around aimlessly before finding herself on Kylie's street and stopping in front of the house. She saw the warm glow of the lights coming from inside and imagined Kylie and Ryan laughing as they played with the Barbie doll. She recalled Ryan's words from the night before—*sometimes Mommy gets lonely and cries.* She knew without a doubt that Kylie was crying now because of her.

"I am treating her like crap," she whispered. Ashamed of her actions, she hung her head but knew she was unwilling to do things differently. "No matter who it hurts? Does it bother me if I hurt Kylie? Yes." Then why was she doing it?

Once again, she looked at the house and knew in the deepest recesses of her soul that she longed to be there. All she'd ever wanted in her life—even as a child—was a place with someone inside who loved her. That desire had become a dream that she held deep inside, refusing to let it emerge. With a heavy ache in her heart, she put her truck in gear before slowly driving away.

She'd call Max and see if she was available. That way she could fantasize that she was with Kylie without risking the emotional involvement.

†

Kylie was sitting on the couch feeling as if she had lost all self-respect from the way she was carrying on over LJ. She couldn't help herself though. Tears were cascading down her cheeks when she heard the sound of a truck. Her heart quickened as she thought maybe, just maybe, LJ was there. She got up, hurried to the door, and peeked out the side window. She saw the familiar truck parked on the street across from her home with what looked like the engine running. The light was poor, but she could make out the silhouette in the driver's seat—unmistakably it was LJ.

Is she going to come to the door? After ten minutes, the truck pulled away, and tears once again rolled down her cheeks in unstoppable rivulets.

"Mommy, why are you crying?" Ryan had come into the living room, where Kylie was now sitting on the couch.

Kylie looked up at her wonderful, loving daughter. "Mommy is just a little sad right now, sweetie."

Ryan scrambled onto the couch and snuggled close to her mother before giving her a big hug and kiss while wrapping her small arms around her neck. "I love you,

Mommy. Please don't be sad."

Kylie hugged Ryan close as the tears increased. "Thank you, Pumpkin, I needed that. What do you say we go to bed early tonight?"

"Want me to stay with you, Mommy?"

"Yes, I would like that very much. I love you, Ryan. Do you know that?"

"Yes."

Kylie stood and held out her hand.

Ryan grasped it as they turned out the lights and went upstairs. "You're the best mommy in the whole world."

Kylie sucked back a sob. "And you are the best daughter ever. I don't know what I'd do without you."

"Mommy, maybe you can have your new friend Lgie come here for a playdate and then you wouldn't be sad anymore."

Out of the mouth of babes. Kylie ruffled Ryan's hair just as they reached the top of the stairs. "Get your jammies on, go to the bathroom, and brush your teeth."

"Okay, Mommy." Ryan hurried to her room. "I'll be right back."

Kylie watched her daughter go and swiped at her tears, wondering if she'd ever stop crying and laugh again. "A playdate with LJ," she whispered. "That is just what I need to get myself out of this funk."

They snuggled in the bed after Kylie read Ryan a story. She closed her eyes and thought of LJ and what she needed to do to bring her around to the possibility of a relationship. She could be persuasive when she put her mind to it. All she needed was a plan. *Shoot, I was going to call Granny tonight.* She looked at the clock, and although it was still early, she was too emotionally exhausted and decided to speak with her tomorrow night.

†

LJ arrived back at her apartment and again considered calling Max but knew that wouldn't solve anything.

She looked around the cold, sterile living room, realizing that was the exact same image she wanted to project to the world. In comparison to Kylie's warm, inviting home, her apartment didn't invite people in. Just the opposite. Not that anyone ever saw her apartment, for she never allowed visitors. Even Max.

"Max. Hmm. I wonder." LJ pulled her phone from her pocket and flicked it on. She yawned and her shoulders fell. Exhaustion overtook the need for sexual release. She hadn't slept the night before, and the day of isolation had been draining in more ways than she'd ever imagined. Her daily struggle not to go to Kylie and hold her close had taken its toll. With the skim of a finger across the phone's screen, she turned it off and headed for her bedroom.

As LJ lay in bed and on the edge of sleep, an image of Kylie floated in her subconscious, and the memory of their lips touching, kissing, and melding into one the night before demanded recognition. LJ's need for Kylie had grown exponentially during the time they'd spent together at her house, and it needed tamping down. There was no way she'd allow herself to become involved. Yet as sleep overtook her, the word *Kylie* drifted from her mouth. In that moment of clarity, she knew in her soul that what she was feeling was so much more than just sexual.

Chapter Twelve

The standoff was into its second week and both women had withdrawn into themselves. Max had shown up twice for what she'd called an "afternoon delight," and LJ was more than willing to accommodate her. The troubling part of Max's visit the day before was her insistence on visiting Kylie to see her progress.

Try as she might, LJ couldn't dissuade Max, who brazenly pushed past her to go to the workroom alone. LJ had stood in the corridor listening and clenching her fingers into a fist, ready to attack if Max tried to treat Kylie unkindly.

To her relief, Max was her usual pleasant, jovial self and sounded genuinely interested in what Kylie was doing. To her ears, Kylie's voice was distant, uninterested, and sad. Knowing she was responsible for it crushed her once again.

When Max returned she asked, "What's wrong with

that woman? Did someone die or something? She's positively depressing." She grabbed LJ's arm. "After being in there I need cheering up, and you are just the woman to do that."

LJ wrenched her arm loose. "Kylie has some personal matters to work out, so don't speak about her like that."

"Well she's downright miserable. Work rules are…number one, never bring your troubles to work; number two, always put on a happy face for visitors. I'd say your little helper has broken both of those rules. No wonder you've locked yourself up in your office. I wouldn't want to be around her with that attitude either."

LJ wanted to scream at Max and tell her she didn't have any right to judge Kylie like that, but she didn't.

Max grinned. "Enough of that. I need you, and I can tell by the look in your eyes you need the same thing."

Max dragged LJ into her office and closed the door. After she flicked the lock, her unrelenting lips were on LJ's, demanding more.

LJ had no fight left in her to resist and gave in to the assault on her body.

When she arrived that morning at four o'clock instead of her usual time, LJ was surprised to find a sealed envelope lying on the floor by the door. She recognized Kylie's distinctive writing and immediately tore open it open and pulled out the note. Her hands were trembling as she read the succinct words.

Dr. Evans,
I have personal business to attend to and will not be

in today. If you want to dock my pay, go ahead and do so.
  Kylie Wilcox

LJ went into panic mode. The note was so formal. Kylie hadn't called her "doctor" since the first few days she'd worked there. *Is she interviewing for another job? Is she quitting and leaving me?* Trying to determine what was happening and what it meant sent an ache through her heart. She walked hurriedly down the hall to the workroom and Kylie's locker. The lock was still there, and that brought her a modicum of relief.

When she was at the worktable, she was amazed at the number of pieces Kylie had finished. Her eyebrows scrunched together while she wondered if Kylie had spent the night there. Surely not; When LJ left she would have seen her.

LJ picked an antiquity up off the table and held it up, visualizing Kylie touching the piece. Holding the object close, as she had with other fragments every morning for the last two weeks, made her feel as if she were touching Kylie. Despair filled her heart. Her well-constructed, solitary life was crumbling around her, and she was powerless to stop it. Truth be told, she welcomed the emotions. They were her punishment for not being there for Holly and now for driving Kylie away.

LJ knew Kylie was leaving. Quitting. She was as certain of that as she was that her heart was crying out for Kylie's warmth. LJ had no one to blame but herself. She left the room still holding the relic—still holding on to Kylie, wondering if she would survive this time.

As she walked down the corridor, she saw Rob coming at her quickly. *Shit, this is all I need.*

"What's going on?" he demanded.

"What are you talking about?" LJ tried to muster some emotion to counter Rob's stern voice but had nothing.

"Why isn't Kylie here today?"

LJ shrugged. "I don't know. I found a note this morning that said she had some personal business to attend to."

"All of a sudden?"

"I guess so. Look, if that's all you want, I'm busy." She looked directly into Rob's eyes that seemed to be appraising her. "I really need to go."

"What's going on with you?"

LJ shook her head. "Nothing."

"I've known you long enough to know that isn't true. Is something going on that I should know about? Does it involve Kylie?"

"No on both accounts."

"I don't believe you. The last time I saw you like this was after Holly died." He reached his hand out, then stopped. "You need to leave the past where it belongs and move on, LJ. There's nothing for you there but heartache," he said in a soft voice.

"Thanks for the advice. I'll take it under advisement. Now, I really need to get back to work."

"You've been mourning for almost fifteen years; it's time to move on and live your life."

LJ looked at the man who had been he champion since her days at the university, knowing the truth behind his words. "I don't know if I can." She shrugged. "Or how to go about doing that."

"Try before it destroys you."

"Can I go now?"

Rob nodded. "Please have Kylie come by my office

when she gets here tomorrow."

"Okay." LJ made a hasty retreat to the solitude of her office. Rob had been too close to the truth, and she needed the distance.

†

At eleven in the morning, the restaurant wasn't very crowded. Lynne waited for Kylie at a table in a secluded corner just as Kylie had requested. She was surprised when Kylie had called and asked if she would have lunch with her.

"Don't you have to work?" she asked.

"Not today" was Kylie's flippant reply.

She knew then that something serious was happening with Kylie. Ted's death hadn't caused her to sound so obviously stressed. Lynne didn't recognize an approaching woman until she'd almost reached the table. When she did, her eyes widened. Kylie looked awful. Her face was drawn, and her eyes were dark and sunken in. Kylie, who didn't need to lose any weight, was as thin as a rail, looking as if she had lost ten or fifteen pounds. Even after Ted had died, Lynne hadn't seen Kylie looking this bad.

"Kylie, what's wrong, has something happened, is it Ryan?" Lynne rose from her seat and embraced her friend.

"What? No. Hello, how ya doin'?" Kylie pulled away.

"Forget me. How are you?" Lynne held Kylie at arm's length and looked her up and down. "No, don't tell me. I can see how you are, and it is not good."

Kylie flopped down into a chair across from where Lynne had been sitting. Her sad eyes gazed at her friend for a long time. "I'm not doing too well, Lynne. Not well at all." She lowered her eyes in what looked like an attempt to stop

145

tears from flowing.

Lynne took her hand. "Want to go somewhere else and talk about it?" Her heart ached for Kylie.

Kylie shook her head. "No. I'll have to force myself to hold it together if I'm in a public place," she whispered.

"You know that with me you can fall apart anytime and I'll be there to hold your hand. Right?"

Kylie nodded. "I know."

The server came to the table. "Do you want anything to drink?"

"She will have a cup of tea, and we both will have the quiche special." Lynne turned back to her friend.

Kylie smiled. "Thank you. I don't think I can handle any decisions at the moment."

"From the looks of it, you haven't been eating at all. Now, tell me, what is going on? Are you sure it's not Ryan, your parents, or your granny? Are any of them sick?"

Kylie shook her head again.

Lynne's mind was in overdrive trying to think of what was going on as tears slowly rolled down Kylie's cheeks. "You're coming up on the anniversary of Ted's passing. Has that got you down?" She was sure that couldn't be it as months ago Kylie had confided in her about the marriage being mediocre at best. Not that Kylie didn't love him—she did—but she said it wasn't the love that songs and romance novels are written about.

"No."

Lynne squeezed the hand tighter, and her voice softened. "Then what is it, Kylie? Please tell me."

Kylie lifted her head. "You know, when I called you, I thought it would be so easy to tell you everything, but right now I can't seem to find the words."

Lynne cocked her head. "Why not start at the

beginning?"

"Once you hear what I have to say, you might not want to be my friend anymore."

Lynne puzzled over the comment. "We have been through a lot over the last twenty-four years. I can't think of anything you could say that would change how I feel about you. Kylie, I love you, and that means nothing you say will make a difference in how I feel." She smiled. "Wasn't it you who got me through that whole debacle when that guy accused me of stalking him?"

Kylie nodded. "Somehow I doubt what I tell you will compare to that in any significant way. I'm sure I'll shock you."

Lynne watched as Kylie's expression changed from sadness to anger, and she used the law of averages to guess what the problem was. "Are you having an affair with a married man and he won't leave his wife for you?"

"Why does everyone always reduce things to a cheap, tawdry affair? If it was that simple, don't you think I would tell you, Lynne?" Kylie growled.

Lynne held up her hand. "Whoa, settle down. I am not the enemy here, Kylie."

The waitress returned with their lunch, giving them some much-needed breathing room as far as Lynne was concerned. After she left, their eyes met, and Lynne could see the pain in the gray ones across from her.

"Please, trust me." Lynne made sure her voice was full of compassion and understanding. "It will stay just between the two of us." Then, in a loving but strong tone, she said, "And don't think for a minute that I am your judge and jury, regardless of what you have to tell me. Far from it—you know me better than that."

For a long time, Kylie just stared at her friend. "I'm

in love," she finally whispered.

Eyeing her friend, Lynne raised an eyebrow. *If this is love, I want no part of it.* "In love, well that's wonderful, right?"

Kylie scratched her head. "Not in this case. I wish it was as simple as a married man."

Lynne reached across the table and squeezed Kylie's hand again. "I'm glad that's not your style. May I ask with whom?"

"My boss."

"And that is a problem because...?" Lynne's eyebrows rose. "The woman we saw at Rusty's?"

Kylie looked intently at her. "I came on to her and she turned me down," she blurted out.

Lynne nodded. "You're telling me that you're in love with a woman?" she asked, louder than she intended. Fortunately, the restaurant wasn't crowded yet, and no one seemed to pay her any attention. Lynne had several gay and lesbian friends, didn't have a problem with their sexuality, and was glad that Kylie had chosen her to confide in. "Are you more upset because of the gender or the fact you were turned down?"

Kylie gave her a slight smile. "Leave it to you to get right down to the core of the problem." She blew out a breath. "Upset about lusting after a woman? Surprisingly it seems rather natural to me. My heart is breaking, Lynne, and I don't know how to stop it." Tears were trickling down her cheeks.

Lynne moved to the chair next to Kylie and put her arm around her. "Why don't you tell me everything and let's see if we can come up with an answer to your problem."

A half smile appeared on the tearstained face. "I would like that. I've spoken to my granny about this, but...."

"You told Granny Mitchell?"

"Yes. She's been very supportive…." Kylie wiped her nose. "I've made a mess of things and didn't want her to know."

"She loves you and never would judge you."

"I know. I just needed to talk to you, Lynne. You've always been there for me and I just need to figure this all out."

Lynne closed her eyes while she collected her thoughts. "Why not start at the beginning?"

Forty-five minutes later, Kylie finished her story.

Lynne took Kylie's hand again. "You are my friend and I love you dearly. Just for the record I don't want you in my bed."

They both laughed, and Lynne knew her friend was back.

"That was two weeks ago, and she hasn't spoken to or seen me since."

Lynne shook her head and smiled. "Have you attempted to see or speak to her?"

Kylie's eyebrows scrunched. "Don't you think from what I've told you that she made it quite clear she doesn't want that?"

She crooked a finger under Kylie's chin before lifting her head so their eyes would meet. "Why are you making her mind up for her? Did she at any time say, 'Don't see me or speak to me'?"

"No, but…."

"No buts about it, Kylie. Give this doctor of yours a chance to tell you. Go talk with her. Tell her how you feel and how much you hurt. If she doesn't know, you can't blame her for how she acts. Just as you can't decide what she's thinking."

Kylie sighed deeply. "Lynne, you're right. I haven't given her a chance. To be honest, I really don't know what she's thinking or how she's feeling. By silently agreeing to her pushing me away, I probably sent her the message that I don't care and am happy with the way things are." Kylie sat there for a moment, seeming to be lost in thought. "Lynne, do you mind if I go now? I have someone very important I need to see." A small, bright smile crossed her face.

Lynne couldn't help but smile back. "You go ahead. Will you let me know what happens?" She squeezed Kylie's hand. "Either way."

Kylie stood, still smiling. "You'll be the first one I call." She bent down and gave her friend a hug. "Thank you, I owe you for this." She began walking away but stopped, then turned back to the table. "Guess it would be nice if I paid since I invited you." She laughed, then put two twenties on the table.

Lynne laughed too. "That's going to be a very generous tip. I think twenty should be enough."

"She left us alone, so she deserves a good tip."

Lynne shook her head and smiled. "You're too much. Go on now and find your answers." She watched as Kylie hurried out of the restaurant on her way to what Lynne hoped would be her future. Yet she worried for her friend.

Although Kylie was enamored with her boss, Lynne wondered if she had considered all the ramifications. Yes, the Supreme Court had declared gay marriage to be legal, but that didn't mean the general population or at least radical sections of it would go along with it. She thought of Kylie's parents who were churchgoers and Republicans, wondering if they would be accepting if their daughter was in a same-sex relationship.

That's a ridiculous, narrow-minded, bigoted thought.

I go to church, am a Republican, and I have no problem with Kylie's choices. She got up to leave. *Just because you're a lesbian doesn't mean you're liberal and vote Democratic.* Off the top of her head, she could think of at least a dozen Republican gay or lesbian celebrities and filed that fact away just in case someone said something about Kylie's possible relationship.

I won't let anyone judge or hurt her. Besides, the most important person in all this if it becomes public is Ryan. There's no doubt that if your kid is anything like you, Kylie, it won't be a problem. Go for it. Love rules. Lynne was grinning as she left the restaurant. She knew her friend would be okay once she expressed her feelings.

†

LJ sat at her desk surrounded by shelves filled with antiquities telling the story of the past and found it amusing that is couldn't help her with the here and now. Rob's words from months before echoed in her mind—*"Did it ever occur to you that you have spent so much time with the dead that you have forgotten how to be human?"* He was right. She had pushed everything and everyone away, leaving her alone and lonely. Even her parents and brothers wanted nothing to do with her.

She was in her first year at the university when she met and fell in love with Holly Brown. Their love dominated her entire being, and LJ was anxious to have her family meet Holly.

Fueled by her happiness and sixteen-year-old naivety, LJ called her parents. She invited them to come and visit so they could meet the special person in her life.

Her mother was happy beyond words that her willful daughter finally had someone and joyfully agreed to the visit. "I've missed you so much," her mother said. "I'm eager to see you again and meet this new person in your life."

When LJ went to her dorm, she was glad to see her parents who were standing in her room with Holly. After hugging them, she went over to Holly and put her arm around her. "Mom, Dad, this is Holly, the love of my life." LJ beamed as she looked at Holly with love.

It never occurred to LJ that her parents would object, but they did. Her mother collapsed in a fit of crying as her father went ballistic. "This is unnatural, and no daughter of mine will be labeled a freak," he shouted.

Her mother cried, "Lucinda Jane, this can't be! You are too intelligent for this," before turning away from her.

Confused by their actions, LJ said, "But I love her; she makes me happy. How is that wrong, and what does my intellect have to do with this?" Holly slipped out of LJ's arms and headed for the door, but LJ grabbed her hand. "Please stay. I need you."

"This will end right now, young lady. You will withdraw from the university and come home with your mother and me," her father ordered.

"I will not! You can't make me." LJ had a death grip on Holly's fingers. "I got here on my own with a scholarship, so you can't tell me what to do."

"You will listen to me and do as I say, or you will no longer be our daughter," Ed Evans threatened.

"Then you have no daughter. Now get out," she growled.

Her mother was now clutching her. "Please, Lucinda Jane, don't do this, I'm begging you." Copious tears coursed down her cheeks.

LJ went to the door and opened it wide, ignoring the students standing in the corridor listening. "Get out now," she screamed, glaring at her parents.

Ed grabbed his wife's arm and escorted her out of the room, sneering at Holly as he passed her. "You've made your bed, little girl, now you sleep in it," he hissed. "You know she's only sixteen. I could have you arrested for rape."

"Nothing has happened," LJ said as she got between her father and Holly. "Just go." She closed the door and leaned against it.

"I'm sorry," Holly said.

"I'm the one who needs to say that. I can't believe my parents acted that way." She sighed. "Had I known, I never would have asked them to come here for a visit."

That night Holly held LJ as she cried for the loss of her family.

LJ had called her mother after Holly died, but heard only coldness instead of sympathy. She recalled her mother saying something like "Good" or "I'm glad" but never could remember the exact words for they hurt too much. She sent them an announcement of her doctorate, but they never acknowledged that either, so she just gave up trying. Only her Grandma Rhodes came to her graduation.

"My dear, I am so proud of you." The old woman hugged her granddaughter and kissed her cheek. "Do you know how much I love you? You've always been my special girl."

"Gran, thank you for coming; it means a lot to me." LJ bent down, hugged the tiny woman again, and breathed in the scent of Lily of the Valley, a smell she always associated with her grandmother.

"I take it your parents didn't come." She looked around them with her face set in an angry expression.

"No. They haven't spoken to me in years, so why would they come now," LJ said sadly.

"It's horrible what they are doing to you." She hugged her granddaughter again. "You will always have a home with me. You know that, don't you?"

LJ nodded and stepped back from the woman she adored. "I took a path they didn't want me to take. It's as simple as that."

"For heaven's sake, love is love. I told them that and how shameful they were to disown you."

"Gran, it is okay. Heck, I have you. You're the best gran ever. How can I lose?" LJ smiled at the small, frail woman.

"You will never be without, Lucinda Jane. I have seen to that."

"Gran, you are wonderful. I need nothing but you." Smiling at the old woman, LJ placed an arm in hers. "What do you say I take my favorite girl out to dinner?"

Six months after that graduation, her grandmother died, leaving her all alone in the world. Her parents attended the funeral and her mother was suitably distraught, but they said nothing to her. Once they found out Marion Rhodes left everything she owned to LJ, her parents contested the will. With no evidence that Marion's judgment was impaired at the time she wrote it, they lost the case. That incident sealed her fate with her parents forever. Clearly all they ever cared about was her grandmother's property and money.

Kylie had tried to care about her, but she'd thrown it

away. She looked at the cookie tin that had sat on the edge of her desk for the last two weeks and pulled it across the desk before opening it. She took out a cookie and took a bite. It melted in her mouth exactly as the one she'd had at Kylie's home did. Her heart sank as she recalled the tears Kylie had shed that night and the next day at work when she heard her quiet sobs.

It seemed to her that Kylie had agreed to their mutual separation because Kylie hadn't protested it. The fact she refused to eat the lunch LJ had delivered every day was another clue that she wanted nothing from her. LJ knew she was responsible for the situation but never anticipated how much it hurt each evening to see the lunch bag sitting untouched. Each time she felt the rejection stabbing at her heart.

Now she had finally run Kylie off, and LJ was at a loss at what to do to make things better.

How very lonely I am. Was she destined to be that way forever without anyone who loved her? She placed her hands over her face, hung her head, stood, and walked a few steps before sliding down the wall to the floor. All the sadness and desolation of a life gone by welled up inside her, and sobs soon turned into a wail for the loss of Holly, her parents, her gran, and the phantom of who Kylie could have been to her. The pain of all the years came to the surface as she realized how isolated she'd become. Kylie had offered her acceptance, kindness, and a chance, yet she had squandered that. Now regret filled her heart. *Why did I sabotage what she was offering me?* Friendship and perhaps more was there right there in front of her, and she hadn't realized what it was until too late.

✝

Kylie parked her car and was glad to see the familiar old truck still parked in the lot. The entire way to the museum, she'd rehearsed what she would say to convince LJ that they should explore a deeper relationship. Lynne had been right—her silence and acceptance of the situation spoke volumes and did not accurately reflect what she felt.

She knew the side door wasn't an option and hoped she could get inside the building without running into Rob. If Lynne's observations were true—she suspected they were— the last thing she wanted to do was explain to the curator why she looked so bad.

Two school buses arrived, and kids began spilling out of the doors. She waited until they were all going up the stairs and merged with them, entering the museum. Once inside, she veered to the left and punched the code for the door that led to the basement.

She skipped down the stairs as fast as she could and practically ran down the corridor to the closed black door. Her heart was pounding when she put her hand on the door, and she frowned crookedly when she heard what she thought were sobs and moans behind it. They sounded much like the wailing of a person who had lost someone dear to them.

LJ? Is she okay? She slowly pushed open the door and listened again. Now she was certain someone was crying and that someone had to be LJ. With quiet steps, she walked inside and took the well-known path to LJ's desk. She stopped in the doorway when she saw LJ hunched over on the floor.

Kylie rushed to her and knelt down by her side. "Oh, LJ, what's wrong?"

LJ looked up. "I'm all alone," she cried.

Kylie sat on the floor and engulfed LJ in her arms.

"You're not alone. I'm here." She kissed the top of her head.

LJ looked up. "Why are you here?"

"I can't stand what is going on between us, and I need to talk to you about it." She rocked LJ gently. "I want you to be happy," she whispered. She held her closer, leaving no space between them.

Kylie didn't know how long they sat there before LJ's tears finally began to subside. She lifted her head and focused her red, swollen eyes on Kylie.

"I thought I'd lost you," LJ said in a raspy voice as her tears began to fall again.

Kylie bent her head and kissed the watery eyes. "I'm not going anywhere." She gently kissed LJ's cheek.

"I'm not sure what I can offer you, Kylie. I feel so lost and empty. Will that be enough for you?"

"What do you say we play this by ear and see what happens? I would like to get to know you as a friend too."

LJ closed her eyes and took a deep breath before she rested her head on Kylie's shoulder. "I would like that too. You know, I've only had one friend in my life, and she died."

"Oh, sweetheart, that is horrible. If you let me, I would like to be your friend." Kylie breathed in LJ's scent and knew in that instant just how right being with her was. The strong, stoic LJ Evans was having a meltdown and was reaching out to her. She vowed always to be there for her. "Hey, what do you say we get up off this cold floor and go somewhere for lunch?"

"Do you mind if we just stay here? I don't think I can face anyone else."

"Of course." Kylie kissed LJ's head. "I bet there's a bag with a salad and sandwich in the workroom we can share."

LJ shook her head. "Not today. You weren't here, so I

canceled the order."

Kylie looked at the desk. "We can have cookies unless you've eaten them all." She grinned. "Considering the circumstances, a lunch of cookies will be just fine."

"They're really good, and no, I haven't eaten them all…only one."

†

While eating cookies, LJ really looked at Kylie for the first time in two weeks and couldn't believe her eyes. Her face was drawn and her body was thinner. "Look at you." She caressed Kylie's cheek.

"My friend Lynne had the same expression on her face when I met her earlier. Do I look that bad?"

"It appears as though you haven't slept or eaten in days," LJ said softly. "Did I do that to you?"

Kylie turned away. "I was such a fool for throwing myself at you, and then when you didn't want to even see me…."

"You didn't make a fool of yourself. I was the one who was running away from what I was feeling for you."

"Why?"

"It's a long story."

"I'm a good listener."

LJ caressed Kylie's cheek. "I'm too raw to tell you, and it would take more energy than I have right now. I will tell you, though, just not today." She let her fingers run circles over Kylie's cheek. "I promise. Is that okay?"

"Of course it is. I understand exactly what you're saying. Isn't it funny how we both came unraveled at the same time?"

"What do you mean?"

158

"I was so miserable with what was going on between us that I had to talk to someone. So I asked one of my best friends to meet me." Kylie smiled. "I told her I was falling for a woman, and she didn't bat an eyelash. She told me if I didn't speak with you and tell you what I was feeling, you had no way of knowing."

"She sounds like a wise friend."

"Yes, she is. That's why I came back, and I'm glad I did."

"I am too." LJ stood. "I guess we'd better get back to work."

"Would you like to come for dinner tonight? Ryan has been asking about her new friend Lgie ever since you were there two weeks ago. I think she's really taken with you." Kylie rubbed LJ's arm softly. "Kids have a way of knowing who is or isn't worth it. Did you know that?"

LJ shook her head. "No. I really don't know much about kids."

"From what I saw when you were with Ryan, you're a natural. Kids have a way of letting adults be one of them."

LJ pulled Kylie closer. "Can we do it another time? I just don't think I'm up to it just yet."

"Of course, just tell me when."

"Kylie, please know I meant it when I said another time. I will not shut you out again. I do want to explore my feelings for you. Right now it's just complicated."

Kylie wrapped her arms around LJ and kissed her lightly on the cheek. "I want that too, and I'm willing to wait for you to be ready as long as I know there is a future."

"There will be." LJ yawned. "I think I could sleep for a week."

"Maybe you should take the rest of the day off and just go home and relax."

LJ grinned and it felt good. "I will if you will."

"Deal."

"Hello, LJ, are you here?" Max's voice echoed from the workroom.

Kylie and LJ rolled their eyes.

"Damn. Why is she here?" LJ grumbled.

Kylie tried to tamp down her jealousy. She knew exactly why Max Dylan was there. "I'll leave you to it, then." She tried to smile, but it didn't reach her eyes. "I think I will take you up on the offer and go home."

"Kylie...."

"It's your life, LJ, and you can—"

"There you are." Max entered the office and looked between the two women. "Oh, am I interrupting something?"

"No, I was just leaving." Kylie looked at LJ. "I'll see you tomorrow." She nodded, then walked toward the door.

"Darling, why are you looking so miserable? Never mind, I'm here now and I'll cheer you up."

"Max, not today."

"What's got you in such a snit? That assistant of yours?"

"Leave it," LJ snapped. "I said today isn't a good time. Will you please leave?"

"You don't mean that," Max protested.

Kylie sucked in a cleansing breath before leaving the room.

LJ took a step backward as Max advanced on her and ran a finger down the cleft between her breasts. "I said stop it!"

Max cocked her head and frowned. "You're serious, aren't you?"

"Yes. Please leave."

Max laughed. "Give me a call when you're over whatever it is."

"Don't come back."

Max shrugged. "Okay. Your loss, but I know you don't mean it." She lifted one side of her mouth in a smug smile. "I saw how your nipples hardened just now. You want me and you *will* call me."

As soon as Max left, LJ pulled her phone out of the back pocket of her jeans and dialed Kylie's number. When Kylie answered, she blurted out, "She's gone. I wanted you to know."

"I know, I'm watching her get in her car."

"Want to come back inside?"

"No. I think we both are too exhausted right now."

"You're probably right. Can I call you later?"

"Yes, I'd like that."

Chapter Thirteen

Kylie walked into the workroom the next day and was surprised to see LJ sitting at the table piecing together what looked like a bowl. She stood there for several minutes as the tender feeling in her heart warmed her all over. LJ was a complicated woman whom she suspected someone had hurt deeply. It would take time to work past all LJ's defenses, but she was willing to wait.

"Does this mean I'm out of a job?"

LJ looked up and grinned. "No. I thought I'd spend the day with you. I missed our time together." Doubt crossed her face. "If that's okay with you."

Kylie walked over to LJ and placed her hands on her shoulders. "That would be more than okay, it would be wonderful." She smiled. "I too missed spending time with you one-on-one."

"Look what I've found here." LJ held up the piece she was reconstructing. "Do you see it?"

Kylie leaned over her shoulder and studied the bowl.

162

"Yes. It's that glyph again, but it's slightly different in some way. I'm just not sure how."

"If you look closely to where the sun is"—she pointed to an area—"you'll see that unlike all the other ones where the sun was at the top, this one is off to the side. What that means is a mystery at this point."

"This is a first, then."

"Yes."

"What is your best guess at what it means?"

"Ah, that's the question of the day. There's clearly a winged being heading for the sun, but the sun is at an angle unlike the others. This is from a Wari' tribe that lived in the highlands of Peru." LJ sat the piece on the table, her eyes bright. "There is every possibility that this was an attempt by a novice at bowl-making. Or…this could be from an offshoot tribe of Wari' yet to be discovered. Imagine what that would mean to the archaeological community."

The excitement emanating from LJ was palpable, and the air in the room crackled with electricity. Kylie, still standing behind LJ, patted her shoulder. "You're going to do it. I can feel it, can't you?"

LJ leaned into Kylie's hands, which were still resting on her shoulders. "You know you are playing with fire, right?"

"I know what I want. I've thought of nothing else for the last two weeks."

LJ rubbed her hand over her face. "Do you have any idea how hard I've tried to resist you?" She blew out a breath. "You're straight, for God's sake." She got off her stool and turned to face Kylie.

"Apparently I didn't get that memo." Kylie grinned. "Truth be told, I've always found women attractive and alluring. They are who draw my attention, not men."

163

"You've thought about them sexually?"

"Not until recently."

"You don't understand. Looking and maybe even fantasizing is completely different from having a sexual relationship." She wrapped Kylie in her arms, pulled her close, and rested her forehead against hers. "The world isn't that accepting."

"I don't care about the world, LJ, I only care about..."

A door in the distance slammed, and Kylie and LJ took a step back.

"Hello, ladies. How are things going?" Rob Ludlow asked as he entered the workroom. "Kylie, I was worried about you when you didn't come in yesterday. Are you okay?"

"I'm fine."

"Come take a look at what we've discovered," LJ said.

Rob's eyes focus on Kylie, and she looked away.

"Are you sure you're okay, Kylie? You look like you're not feeling well." He glared at LJ. "What's going on here?"

Kylie approached the curator. "Rob, I've had a bug or something for a few days, but I'm all better now. LJ was just trying to convince me that I should go home, and I was telling her I'm fine."

"You really should go home." LJ turned to Rob. "She took the day yesterday, but I was just telling her to go rest until she's completely over whatever she has." She lifted her arms in a gesture of helplessness. "She won't listen."

"Young lady, we can't have one of our employees infect everyone in the museum, so I want you to leave right now and don't come back until you're better," Rob said with a stern expression. "You look awful."

Kylie bowed her head. "I suddenly began feeling much better yesterday afternoon." She lifted her eyes and saw a smirk on LJ's face. "I don't have a fever, and if we're going to figure out this possible new branch of the Wari' tribe, I have a lot of work to do."

Rob's eyes widened. "A new group?"

Apparently her physical well-being was no longer a concern as he focused in on the artifacts LJ held in her hands.

"I think it's a distinct possibility. Let me show what we found."

Kylie stood next to LJ and listened to the cadence of her rich voice as she enthusiastically explained what it was and why it was significant. LJ's heady smell flowed through her senses, making her wish Rob would leave. What she now recognized as desire was creeping through her body, and she would no longer deny it.

LJ watched as Rob left the area and waited until she heard the door shut before looking at Kylie. "You are bad."

Kylie touched her chest. "Me? Why?"

"I saw that look in your eyes, and it's a good thing Rob's attention was elsewhere."

"What look would that be?"

"Kylie, are you sure this is what you want?"

"I've never been surer of anything in my life. The question for me is…what do *you* want?"

With a tenderness she didn't know she still had, LJ kissed Kylie. "Does that answer your question?"

"Not sure. I think you need to explore it further." Kylie cupped LJ's face and kissed her.

LJ pulled away. A multitude of conflicting thoughts and feelings were bombarding her from all directions. She

Erin O'Reilly

wanted Kylie in a way that was foreign to her. Yet it seemed so right. Kylie was offering her a lifeline, and all she had to do was to reach out and take hold.

Kylie took her hand and gave it a gentle squeeze. "I can see all the wheels spinning in that pretty head of yours. Tell me what you're thinking. Maybe I can help."

"What you're offering me is confusing and overwhelming, and I'm trying to get my head around everything I'm feeling." LJ's heart was racing.

"Like what?"

"Desire." She lifted a shoulder. "Terror mainly."

"You're afraid of me?"

"I'm terrified of how much I want you...need you."

"And you think I'm not? This is all new to me, but the rightness of it is too compelling to ignore. I know now that I was trying to rush things with you. What do you say to us taking it slow and seeing where we go from there?"

LJ blew out a breath. "That sounds wonderful to me."

Kylie smiled. "Good. So what do you think about having dinner with us tonight?"

"I'd like that." LJ could feel her heart thawing a little more. "I suppose that means Barbie will be there."

"Afraid so." Kiley leaned in and kissed her before stepping back. "There is also the possibility of more kisses."

"With an offer like that, how can I say *no*?"

"Great." Kiley smiled broadly.

LJ locked her gaze with Kylie's, and the sensation of happily drowning in the pools of gray warmed her body. "I guess we should get back to work."

"Yeah, I guess so. Maybe we'll find that new glyph again if we concentrate in that same area."

"That means we'll be working side by side. Can you handle that?" LJ winked at Kylie.

166

"Oh, I'll try, that's the best I can do."

For the next three hours, LJ sat contently next to Kylie.

†

"Dinner will be ready in ten minutes. You two need to wash up," Kylie called up the stairs.

"Mom, we are having fun."

"Yeah, Mom, we're having fun," LJ echoed, sounding amused.

"Act like the adult, LJ." Kylie laughed as she walked back into the kitchen. After finishing work and going home to prepare dinner, she waited in anticipation for LJ's arrival. The woman who showed up at her door wasn't the coldhearted person she'd met when she started working at the museum. This LJ was relaxed and open, just as she'd been when they worked together that morning.

"What can I do to help?"

Startled, Kylie turned and saw LJ standing right beside her. "Oh." She held a hand to her heart. "I didn't hear you come in." Her eyes tracked over LJ's shoulder. "Where's Ryan?"

"Washing up." LJ pulled her close. "I was faster so I could have a few minutes alone with you."

"You did, did you? What exactly did you have in mind?"

LJ shrugged. "Hugging you and feeling you close to me. It wasn't until I thought I lost you that I realized just how much I needed you."

Surprised by the openness of the comment, Kylie caressed LJ's cheek and smiled before hearing Ryan bound down the stairs. "At least she'll never sneak up on us."

167

LJ let her arms drop. "Want me to set the table?"

"Nope, already done."

"Mommy, can Lgie stay the night?"

"We're lucky we got her to come for dinner. Let's not push our luck, sweetheart."

"Sorry I can't tonight." LJ knelt to be at eye level with the small girl. "Would it be okay if I spend the night some other time?"

"I want you to stay tonight." Ryan stomped her foot and crossed her arms over her chest.

"None of that, young lady," Kylie cautioned.

"But, I want Lgie to play with me some more."

Kylie wiggled her eyebrows. "So do I." She winked at LJ.

"Promise, I'll spend the night sometime and we will play with Barbie some more."

Ryan wrapped her arms around LJ's neck. "You can be Ken next time."

†

LJ listened to the voices that drifted down the stairs and smiled. For the first time since her self-imposed exile from Kylie, she was relaxed. The feeling bubbled up inside her, and even if she wanted to, she couldn't stop the happiness flooding her. Having a family was something she had never considered. But after being with Kylie and Ryan in their home, LJ knew she was exactly where she belonged. However, a modicum of fear and doubt still hid in her heart, refusing to go away.

She had warred with herself and sought out the affections of others to try to forget her fascination with Kylie, even though she knew it was more than a physical attraction.

It was a bone-deep need she had buried so well since Holly's death that she'd forgotten it existed. Once Kylie came into her life, that need began clamoring to break free and see the light of day.

Can I take that chance? Could she allow herself a measure of happiness and risk heartbreak again? She looked up, saw Kylie coming down the stairs, and had her answer.

"Come sit with me." LJ patted the couch cushion next to her.

Kylie sat so their thighs were touching and rested her head on LJ's shoulder. "Is this okay?"

"Perfect." LJ lifted her arm, put it around Kylie's shoulders, and pulled her closer. "Thank you. The meal was delicious."

Kylie laughed. "We both ate like we hadn't eaten in weeks."

LJ lifted and eyebrow. "I don't think we had."

"You're right about that. Thank you."

"For what?"

"Being here with me."

LJ felt Kylie tremble and looked at her. "There is nowhere else I want to be." She stroked Kylie's cheek. "I'd like to kiss you."

"I won't throw myself at you this time."

LJ swallowed hard. The annoying monologue that had constantly been in her head warning her of impending disaster since meeting Kylie found its voice again. "I don't know if I'm ready for more than kissing," she whispered.

"Not a problem." Kylie kissed her cheek. "Despite what happened the last time you were here, I don't think I'm ready for more either. My body might be, but I think we have a lot to talk about first. I want it to be the right place at the right time."

169

LJ could feel her body relax before she leaned in to Kylie's lips and kissed them long and slow. All her pent-up emotions were in that kiss, and despite her misgivings she knew what was happening between her and Kylie was exactly as it should be. She pulled away when Kylie moaned. "I think we better stop now."

"Aw. Can't we kiss a little longer?"

"You look just like Ryan when she pouts." LJ tapped her on the nose.

"Your kisses make me feel things in my body that I had no idea existed, and I want more." Kylie looked at her. "More kisses, nothing else. Promise."

"Yes." LJ leaned in and captured Kylie's lips again.

That night when LJ went home it was with a sense of hope and a belief that she had a future.

Chapter Fourteen

"Did you get the cooler?" LJ asked.

"Yep, it's in the backseat next to where Ryan is sitting."

LJ leaned into the car and looked at Ryan. "You're in charge of the cooler, so make sure it stays put."

"I will, and if you or my mommy needs a drink, I can get it for you."

"Thanks. You're a good helper." LJ stood and surveyed the back of Kylie's SUV. "That seems like an awful lot of stuff to take just to go on a picnic at the zoo."

"And how many picnics to the zoo with an almost-seven-year-old have you gone on to know this?"

With a hearty laugh, LJ gave Kylie a quick hug. "When you're in the jungle on a dig, it's like one great big picnic."

"When are we going?" Ryan whined from inside the SUV.

"Right now, sweetheart." Kylie went around the

vehicle and got inside. "Everyone buckled in?"

"Can we just go?" Ryan asked.

"You buckled in?" Kylie gave Ryan her sternest look. "Buckle in or we don't go."

"Okay, Mommy."

When she heard the click of the seat belt, Kylie said, "Then let's go to the zoo."

†

"Come on, Lgie, let's go see the monkeys." Ryan grabbed LJ's hand and took off for the monkey house.

Kylie laughed and followed them down the concrete path toward an enclosure where monkeys were swinging across the top. When she caught up with them, Kylie couldn't help but notice the look of awe on LJ's face. Ryan was mimicking a monkey by scratching at her armpits and bouncing.

"Hey, Monkey, are you having fun?"

Ryan and LJ looked at her.

"Are you asking this monkey?" LJ tapped Ryan's head.

"Actually I was asking both of you."

"I'll have you know I am not a monkey, but I do find them fascinating."

Ryan grabbed Kylie's hand. "Come on, Lgie, I can see the elephants." She took LJ's hand too and began walking away with them following her.

An hour later, Ryan was in the petting zoo feeding a baby goat.

"Are you having a good time?"

LJ nodded. "Yes. I've never been to a zoo before, so this is all new to me."

"Wait. You've never been to a zoo?"

"No."

Kylie's eyes widened. "You never went on a field trip in grade school to the zoo? I find that impossible to believe."

"I went to a private school that emphasized learning and little else." LJ shrugged.

"What kind of school is that if they don't let kids have the full range of experiences?"

LJ looked away.

"What?"

"I had special needs."

Kylie frowned. "You had special needs. Really?"

Ryan came bounding up to them. "Mommy, I'm hungry."

"Then let's go get the things out of the car and have our picnic." She looked at LJ. "Special needs, indeed. Pull the other one."

†

LJ lay back on the blanket and looked at the blue sky. She had never considered things like the zoo or picnics. Her life was wholly dedicated to her work. Yet here she was at the zoo sharing a picnic with Kylie and Ryan. Being there was surreal but seemed so natural. She looked at the mother and daughter, who appeared to be in a serious conversation. Warmth and contentment flowed around her heart, and for the first time in way too many years, she was happy. The little voice that kept her terrified of any romantic interactions was quiet now, and for that, she was grateful.

"You okay?"

LJ lifted her head and saw Kylie looking at her with concern.

"It seemed like you were miles away."

"I was just thinking about"—she wanted to say "the glyph" but knew it was a lie—"how much I am enjoying this day."

Kylie's face lit up.

"I can't think of anyone else I'd rather be here with than you and Ryan."

"We still have to see the big cats, and don't forget the reptiles." Kylie grinned.

"Snakes and bugs. I'll think I'm back in the jungle."

Kylie laughed. "Someday you will have to tell me all about your adventures."

LJ could see the sincerity in Kylie's eyes along with warmth that she knew was only for her. "Maybe you'll go along on the next dig and find out firsthand."

"I already know it isn't glamorous, but I think being there with you would be a whole different experience from what I had on the digs I went on in college."

"Who was the professor that led the group?"

"Evan Harvey."

LJ nodded. "I know him. He's a decent scholar but"—she grinned—"I'm better."

"I recognized that fact the first day we met."

"Mommy, when are we going back to see the rest of the animals?" Ryan asked.

"Just as soon as we get all this stuff back in the car."

LJ began collecting the picnic paraphernalia while Kylie put the food back in the cooler. "Ryan, will you carry this for me?" She held out the blanket.

Soon they were back at the zoo proper and watched as a leopard paced in its enclosure. Ryan was leaning against the fence, seemingly mesmerized by the big cat.

"On one of the digs a panther wandered into the

174

camp, sniffed the air, looked around, and then walked away. It was awesome," LJ quietly told Kylie.

"Were you scared?"

"Yes, but not of the panther. I was afraid someone would do something stupid and provoke it into attacking."

"Does anything scare you?"

LJ swallowed hard. "Yes. You."

Kylie's eyes went wide. "Me? Why?"

"I'm terrified by what I feel for you."

"Mommy, Lgie, come on, I see the giraffes."

"We will discuss this further," Kylie said before Ryan grabbed her hand.

†

The day at the zoo had been one of the most relaxing times of LJ's life. She was sitting on the grass in Kylie's backyard watching fireflies lift from the ground and do their mating dance. When she was younger that sort of thing fascinated her, but she'd lost her way. Now, looking at the flickering lights, she smiled.

"Hey, mind if I join you?"

LJ patted the grass next to her. "Did she finally go to sleep?"

"Yes. She was quite upset that you didn't stay until she did."

"I was being too much of a distraction."

Kylie laughed and sat right next to LJ. "Yes, you were. I swear you must be a kid at heart with the way you two have bonded."

"She's a good kid."

Kylie rested her head on LJ's shoulder. "I really liked the person you were today at the zoo. You should let her out more often."

LJ felt her lips on her cheek and leaned into them.

"You said you went to a special-needs school and that I terrified you. Will you please tell me why?" Kylie asked quietly.

"All my life growing up, I was the odd girl out."

"What do you mean?"

"I never seemed to fit in anywhere. Except...." The arm that went around her shoulders made her shiver. "You see those fireflies?"

"Yes."

"They light up to find a mate, and after reproducing they die. I've often wondered if when one dies, the other one dies too."

"You mean like they are soulmates or something?"

"Yes. Eagles mate for life, so why not fireflies? They just live for one mate and no other."

"I suppose that's possible, but I doubt it."

LJ shrugged. "Is that how you felt after you lost your husband?"

"I never thought of him as my soulmate."

"Why not?"

"He was controlling and manipulative."

"Why'd you marry him, then?"

"It was what was expected. Get married, have kids, and live happily ever after. And my parents were so happy when I started dating Ted that I didn't want to disappoint them." Kylie wrapped her arms around her knees. "I loved him for a time until I found out it was a lie. I had made a vow of forever and had to keep that. So I was stuck."

"Were you happy?"

"Not really. But that isn't important right now. Why did you feel like that growing up?"

LJ could feel Kylie's eyes on her and knew she wasn't getting away with deflecting the question.

"You said you never fit in 'except' and didn't finish the sentence. Please tell me what else you were going to say."

"We met at the university as roommates." LJ poured her heart out, telling Kylie about Holly and that when her life ended, so did LJ's.

"Oh, LJ, how horrible for you." Kylie put an arm around her shoulders. "What can I do to help you?"

LJ couldn't stop the streams of tears that rolled down her cheeks. "Every time I'm with anyone else, I feel like I'm cheating on her," she whispered.

"From what you've said about Holly, it sounds like she was a kind, warm, and loving person who wasn't clingy or demanding. Do you really think she'd want you to resign from life or love and build a temple to her memory?"

"I haven't done that," LJ growled.

"Haven't you?"

LJ looked away. "I thought that is what I wanted."

"And now?"

"Today with you and Ryan…I realized you are who I want. I recognized there was more to life. I want a family that will love me and accept me for who I am."

"Where's your family?" Kylie pulled her into warm, loving arms.

"I can't go there right now. It's been a long and very emotional day. Do you mind?"

"No. Whenever you're ready, I'm here to listen without judgment. Can you tell me why you were in a remedial class in school?"

"I never used the word *remedial*. I said 'special needs.'"

Kylie frowned. "From what I can tell, you don't have any handicaps."

"A special need doesn't just include disabilities, Kylie." LJ blew out a breath. "The school I went to catered to students with an IQ in the upper two percent of the population."

"What is your IQ?"

LJ looked away. "One hundred and sixty-seven."

"Wow. Am I getting this right? If you have a high IQ you aren't allowed to go to the zoo or on field trips?"

"We went on field trips, but they weren't geared to children but adults."

Kylie caressed her cheek. "That makes me sad for you."

"Why?"

"You missed out on all the fun of being a kid."

"I couldn't miss something I didn't have a clue about. To me it seemed perfectly normal."

"And lonely."

LJ nodded. "Perhaps after what we did today…yes."

Kylie hugged her closer. "Not anymore."

LJ caressed Kylie's cheek and felt her lean in to the touch. It would be so easy to kiss the tempting lips she'd longed to feel on hers all day. She moved away. The light was dim, but her eyes had adjusted and she could see desire reflecting back at her. "I can't."

"Why?"

"Because I want you so much that it scares me, and I don't know if I can go there again."

"But you can with Max or that singer."

"That's different. They're just a fuck." She pulled her close. "You are not." LJ kissed her gently before moving away. "Please just hold me a little while."

"Will you at least spend the night?"

"I can't."

"The spare bedroom is all made up, and I promise not to throw myself at you."

LJ shook her head. "It's not that. I…I don't trust myself not to visit you in the night."

"That would be okay." Kylie grinned, then winked at LJ.

"No, it wouldn't." She took Kylie's hand. "Don't you see that you deserve more than one night of passion, and right now that is all I can give you?"

Kylie wrapped her arms around LJ. "I want more than that too. You do remember that you promised Ryan you would spend the night? Tonight might be the perfect time." Kylie wiggled her eyebrows.

LJ sucked in an audible breath. "As tempting as that sounds I have to pass. I'm sorry."

"Don't be sorry. Like you said, when the time is right, we'll both know it."

There in the dark sitting on the grass and holding each other with fireflies glowing all around them, Kylie could feel her world righting. She'd give LJ all the room she needed, for there was nothing in her life that had ever felt so perfect.

Chapter Fifteen

Kylie sat across from LJ at the worktable and looked at the woman hunched over a magnifying glass looking at pottery pieces. To the world, LJ was a cold, dour, unapproachable woman. To her and Ryan, she was tender, kind, and warm. *If only the rest of the world could see you the way I do.* At that thought, Kylie began to formulate a plan.

They had been working side by side during the day and spending the evenings together. It surprised her how easily LJ adapted to the home-cooked meals and the company of both herself and Ryan.

LJ had told her that for most of her life, she was a loner who relied only on herself, so Kylie knew her willingness to join them was a complete reversal for her. At first, LJ was tentative in being a part of their life, but it didn't take her long to fully integrate into the mother-and-daughter family

"LJ?"

"Hmm."

"I would like you to meet my friends Lynne and Jodie."

LJ looked up. "They're the ones you were with that night at the Rusty Nail?"

"Yes. They've been my friends for years, and I know they'll like you."

"Oh, I'm not sure about that." LJ looked away. "You know I don't do well around strangers. Look how long it took me to relax around you."

"They are just like me...an extension, really."

"Kylie, I just can't."

"Please."

LJ looked at Kylie and wished she hadn't. The gray eyes pleading with her were her undoing. "Don't ask me like that."

"Don't you know I want the whole world to know how wonderful and warm you are?"

"Don't you know I'm not a people person?"

"Yes, you are. You just choose not to show it."

"Kylie...please don't ask me to go out with your friends. I don't want to embarrass you."

"Never. I'm proud of you and being with you. Please. For me. I promise if it gets too uncomfortable for you, all you have to do is say so and we'll leave right away."

LJ let out a long sigh. "Since you asked so nicely, okay, I'll go."

Kylie flew around the table, wrapped LJ in her arms, and kissed her cheek. "Thank you. I promise you'll have a great time."

"I guess I'll find out, won't I?"

†

That evening Ryan was at her grandparents' and LJ was going out with Kylie to join Lynne and Jodie for dinner. She recalled the conversation earlier that day and her regret at saying yes to the "date" as Kylie called it…

"They are no different than anyone else. You'll like them, I promise."

"I don't know. How should I act? What if they discover that we might be more than friends?"

"First of all, Lynne already knows how I feel about you, and Jodie is cool with almost everything."

"It's that word *almost* that has me worried."

Kylie hugged her close and kissed her cheek. "She isn't like that."

"Do you know the last time I went out to dinner with anyone socially?"

"No, when?"

"When I got my doctorate, I took my grandmother out to dinner. That was twelve years ago."

"Certainly you've gone to museum functions since then." Kylie pulled her in closer.

"Those weren't social events. They were mandatory, and I went, had the meal, shook some hands, and left as soon as I could. I don't do well in social situations, I told you that. Why I agreed to this I'll never know."

Kylie stepped back and frowned. "Someday you will have to tell me who did this to you."

"Did what?"

"Made you feel unworthy, like an outcast."

The last thing LJ wanted to do was discuss her family. "Fine, I'm going to dinner with you and your friends, and I will try to be sociable."

A brilliant smiled curved Kylie's lips. "It's our first date out in public. When was the last time you were on a date?"

Embarrassed, LJ looked away. "Not since I lost Holly."

"Well that is about to change." Kylie kissed her lips softly. "This will be the first of many such times. I promise you that."

Now she was standing in front of the small medicine cabinet mirror, trying to get a look at her outfit. She had never really cared about what she wore. For her a pair of jeans, a long-sleeve shirt, sturdy boots, and a snug-fitting jacket were all she needed for the work she did. In order to see herself, she had to stand on the tub wall and found she was only able to see the white silk shirt tucked into her black slacks. It was the only outfit she had for going to functions.

"This is for the birds. I'm just going to put on what is comfortable and the hell with dressing to impress." LJ began unbuttoning the shirt, then stopped. The night was important to Kylie and she desperately wanted her to be happy. "Fine, I'll wear this."

She rummaged around in her closet and found a pair of black boots that she thought would look good with the outfit. There was no way she was going to wear the heels she'd worn at the last function Rob insisted she attend. It was a fundraiser for her dig to Peru, so she had to go and be sociable and not decline the invitation, as was her usual tactic. The heels had been a last minute concession to the importance of the event. Rob had told her that she needed to impress the possible donors and to dress accordingly. That decision was a mistake as her feet had hurt for days afterward.

"The boots are serviceable and are polished. They will have to do." She slipped them on, looked down at her attire, and closed her eyes. "What have I gotten myself into?"

With truck keys in hand, she left her apartment to pick up Kylie before going to the restaurant.

†

LJ tugged at the sleeve of her jacket and took it off before sitting in a chair at the upscale restaurant. She looked nervously at Kylie, who was hugging her best friends. For a moment, she longed to have Kylie hug her to help squelch the uncertainty she was feeling.

Lynne was blonde with deep blue eyes and stood around five two with a body that looked as if she'd been a gymnast at one time. Jodie was tall with long, brown hair and chocolate-brown eyes, and although she wasn't as trim as Lynne, she had a decent body. They both had been welcoming when they met her.

They settled into the night together with drinks, and soon the three women started to chatter as LJ had heard others do. Not ever having friends, she didn't quite understand this ritual and was glad no one seemed to pay her any attention.

"Kylie tells me you are the chief research archaeologist at the museum, LJ. That's quite impressive." Jodie cocked her head to the right. "So what are you? Around thirty-five?"

LJ looked at Jodie after she realized one of Kylie's

friends was asking her a question. "Does it matter?" LJ asked defensively. *Coming here was an extremely bad idea.* "You didn't tell me this was going to be an inquisition." She looked pointedly at Kylie before scooting her chair back and getting up.

"No. I didn't mean anything like that. I was just thinking to be where you are at thirty-five it is a wonderful achievement," Jodie spluttered.

LJ glared at Kylie again and walked away at a fast pace.

"She doesn't do well in social settings. I'll go get her and we'll be right back." Kylie got up and walked quickly after LJ. When she caught up to her, she grabbed her hand. "Wait up. What's the matter?" She dragged LJ to a secluded corner of the bar.

"You told me that they weren't going to be judgmental and intrude into my life." LJ motioned back at the table. "So why did you lie to me?"

Kylie could feel not only the anger all around LJ, but fear. "They are my friends, and they know how I feel about you and are trying to get to know you, LJ. There's nothing more than that." She purposely kept her voice soft so LJ would have to lean in to hear her over the noise of the bar. "Would you rather we just talk among ourselves and ignore you?"

"Yes." Defiance colored LJ's tone.

"That's a load of crap and you know it." Kylie caressed LJ's cheek. "I need you to give them a chance. They are my oldest friends, and I want us all to get along because you are in my life and I'm not letting you go."

"You can't say that. You can't control all situations.

All you can do is cope with what you are given."

Eyes that seemed to be full of anxiety were searching hers, and Kylie leaned in and pulled her close. "Trust me. I won't let you fall. I promise," she whispered. "I've got your back."

"I don't know if I can."

"Please try."

LJ took her hand and squeezed it. "For you I will try to be friendly, but there are no guarantees."

LJ was at odds with what she was feeling for Kylie and the terror that was gripping her heart. With Holly everything just seemed to work; although she knew that wasn't always the case, it was what she chose to remember. Kylie was different. On one hand, she desperately wanted what Kylie was offering, and on the other old memories and fears kept trying to resurface. The pleading in Kylie's eyes was her undoing.

"I guess I overreacted." LJ closed her eyes, then opened them to find Kylie smiling.

"Just a little. Fortunately for you, Lynne and Jodie are pretty easygoing, and I know many stories of them making similar scenes, so you're safe on that front."

LJ nodded, took Kylie's hand, and headed back to the table. Kylie's friends looked at her expectantly as they sat down. Not skipping a beat, she said, "Actually I'm almost thirty-three."

Jodie gaped. "When did you get your doctorate?"

LJ swallowed hard and blew out a breath. "When I was twenty."

"You were a child prodigy?" Lynne asked.

"I always thought of it as odd girl out." LJ shook her

head, reminding herself that she'd said she'd try to be more sociable. "I went to a special school that catered to so-called gifted kids. It wasn't the typical school experience."

"In what way?" Lynne asked.

"Okay, enough of the inquisition." Kylie smiled at her friends. "We can all concede that LJ is brilliant."

"That's an understatement," Jodie said. "Who'd like another beer?"

After that, LJ settled down and listened to the chatter between the friends. She realized she had missed so much by isolating herself from other people. She was jealous of what Kylie had with the two women. LJ was so deep in thought, she surprised when her dinner plate arrived in front of her.

Kylie leaned in. "Are you okay?"

"Not really," she whispered.

"Why?"

"Not important." LJ smiled and cut into her steak before taking a bite. What she was feeling wasn't significant. She had a friend now in Kylie, and maybe someday she'd be friends with the other two women. Time would tell.

The rest of the evening was full of laughs, and LJ found herself drawn into the conversation. Lynne and Jodie weren't judgmental and seemed to accept that she and Kylie might become a couple. She even related some stories of hacking through the jungle to get to a dig site and was pleased they were interested and even laughed.

The night was ending, and LJ was grateful. She wanted to get out of there and back to the safety of her truck. The feeling of impending doom had faded, and although she did enjoy herself, she found no comfort in the company of the others. Only Kylie filled the chasm that until then had been a barren wasteland of loneliness. If only she could let down her defenses enough to let Kylie inside completely.

"This was fun," Lynne said. "Let's do it again."

LJ smiled. "I'd like that." She took a deep breath. "I'm sorry I got a little grumpy at the start." She looked down at the table, refusing to make eye contact with anyone.

"Hey," Lynne said, patting her shoulder. "If you ask Kylie, she can tell you stories of my indiscretions out in public."

Kylie laughed. "And in private."

"That too." Lynne squeezed LJ's shoulder. "I'm happy for you and my friend Kylie. She's a keeper," she whispered. "I've never seen her happier."

"What about when she was married?" LJ knew curiosity was getting the better of her, but she didn't care. She wanted to know.

"Oh God, no. At first she was the blushing bride, but that faded quickly."

LJ looked at Kylie, who had returned to speaking with Jodie. Both were laughing and oblivious to her conversation with Lynne. "Thank you for telling me that."

"Telling you what?" Kylie's focus was suddenly on her.

"That you are happy."

Kylie clutched her hand. "I truly am for the first time in my life," she whispered.

For a moment with Kylie's hand on hers and Kylie's eyes focused on her, LJ felt as though no one else was there. She smiled as her heart soared.

†

"Ryan is spending the night with my parents, so why don't you spend the night with me?" Kylie unlocked the front door and walked inside. When LJ didn't follow, she turned and looked at her.

"What?"

"I'd like it very much if you spent the night with me in my bed."

"Kylie, I can't."

"Why? Am I that repulsive to you?"

LJ stepped inside. "Oh God, no. Why do you keep saying that? I've told you repeatedly that it isn't you but me. You are amazing. I want...I want to sleep with you more than anything, but just not yet."

Kylie swiped at the tears brimming in her eyes. "I don't understand. Do you want me to be more like Max or even Cassie?"

"No. Never. You know that. Neither of them can hold a candle to you." LJ wrapped her arms around Kylie. "When I make love...we make love...it will be forever, and that time needs to be special and not some convenient romp in a bed."

"Don't you think I'm scared too? My only sexual experience was with Ted, and it didn't take me long to discover that most of the time it was one-sided."

"All the more reason to take it slow and be certain I am who you want in your bed."

"Haven't you been listening? I want to know you. All of you."

"When I give myself to you, I want it to be all of me, and I'm not there yet," LJ whispered. She lifted Kylie's chin and rubbed a finger over her lips. "Will you wait for me?"

"I have no choice. I've never wanted anything as much as I want to be with you, and I will wait for as long as it takes."

LJ leaned in and kissed Kylie's lips softly. "I'd better get going. I really had fun tonight with your friends. Sorry I was such a pain at the start."

"You weren't a pain. I think you were so far out of your element that it scared you."

LJ lifted an eyebrow. "You ever think of going into psychology?"

Kylie kissed her again. "Don't go. Stay. We'll just sleep, that's all."

LJ shook her head. "I don't trust myself to be that near to you and just sleep."

"Then don't."

"You're incorrigible." LJ shook her head. "I'd better get going."

"If you stay, then we could have a leisurely breakfast in the morning before going to pick up Ryan. You could meet my parents." LJ stiffened. "What?"

"I'm not ready for the parent thing yet." She took a step back. "I need to go."

"Okay, I understand, but at some point you're going to have to meet them."

"I know. Is it okay if I call late tomorrow morning? Maybe we can take Ryan to the park."

"Okay. She'd like that. You are her favorite playmate."

LJ smiled, then turned away.

Kylie watched her get into her truck and drive away. Her phone rang.

"Hello."

"Am I interrupting anything by calling?"

"Hi, Lynne. No, unfortunately you aren't interrupting anything. LJ just left."

"I really like her, Kyl. It took her a bit to warm up to us, but after that I could see what you see in her."

"I've never felt like this about anyone, Lynne. It's like she's reached in and stolen my heart and put a spell on me."

"I could see in the way she looked at you she feels the same way."

"Really?"

"Yes. It's written all over her face. And the sexual fireworks that were coming off the two of you were sooo hot."

Kylie's face heated. "You're just saying that to embarrass me."

"Maybe a little bit, but the chemistry was definitely there."

"She's gorgeous, isn't she?"

"Smokin'. So why aren't you two taking advantage of Ryan not being there?"

"It's complicated. She has a lot of baggage."

"I would imagine so. She couldn't have had much of a childhood if she got her PhD at twenty. No wonder you said she didn't have many social skills. I wonder if she ever got to play with kids her own age."

"Good question. I know when we went to the zoo a few weeks ago, it was a first for her. I can't imagine what it must have been like for her."

"It was probably all she knew, so it was normal for her."

"You're probably right. As I unravel the mystery of LJ Evans, I will have to find out the answer to what makes her tick."

"Be careful. If you delve too deeply, you may find more than you can handle."

"She's worth it."

"You've really got it bad, don't you?"

"Yes." Kylie yawned. "Listen, it's been a long day, and I'm having a hard time keeping my eyes open."

Lynne laughed. "I bet if she was there you wouldn't be saying that."

"Probably not."

"Okay. Have a good night and give me a call on Sunday and we can arrange a day for lunch next week."

"I will. Good night, Lynne."

"Good night."

Kylie ended the call and yawned again. It had been a long week. She locked up and headed up to her bedroom, wishing LJ was there with her.

Chapter Sixteen

Over the next month, LJ spent more time with Kylie and Ryan. They shared dinners and went to the park every Saturday so Ryan could swing and climb on the monkey bars. One day as they sat watching Ryan hang upside down on the monkey bars, she realized in amazement how much she doted on the child. Kids generally annoyed her. But something about the girl's easy nature made her want to watch over her and protect her.

As much as she enjoyed the family time, LJ made certain she and Kylie went out on dates at least twice a week. At work, she found herself longing to touch Kylie, and it took every ounce of her determination not to. While examining artifacts she could feel the heat coming from Kylie along with the scent of a sweet spring morning that she came to associate with the woman.

Yet she resisted the voice that called to her to take the plunge and commit fully to Kylie, with whom she knew she was falling in love. Old fears and memories still haunted her, and until she could resolve those, she'd stay rooted in place. That didn't stop her from taking every opportunity she could to be with or around Kylie. She couldn't get enough of and did not intend giving her up ever.

That morning, when Kylie began piecing together what looked like a promising clue to the glyph, LJ leaned in so close that their cheeks were a whisper apart. When she rested her hand on Kylie's shoulder, she could feel her tremble, and she reacted the same way. The attraction was becoming undeniable, and she moved away to distance herself in an attempt to squelch her burgeoning emotions.

Instead of spending the morning as she usually did with Kylie, she had made a hasty retreat to the safety and solitude of her office. It was becoming more difficult to contain her need to be with Kylie on a more intimate level. She knew the time was coming when she'd resist no more. The question then became would she continue to stay stubbornly in the past or move on to what she knew was her future?

✝

Kylie watched LJ leave and sighed. They had agreed to refrain from being intimate until they were both sure it was what they wanted. Kylie knew in her heart what was right, but she also knew LJ was fragile and therefore they needed to go slow. Only moments ago LJ had rested a hand on her shoulder before leaning in so close that Kylie had to close her eyes. She tried to will her heart to stop from beating at a rate she was sure might make it explode. Going to the next level was becoming a deep, burning need for her.

She shook her head before looking back at what appeared to be a plaque or picture of some sort that she had been trying to piece together all morning. Hours later, it was finally beginning to take shape. The more parts she added, the possibilities became clearer that it might be the key to the mystery LJ was trying to solve. Lying on the table in front of her, the picture appeared to contain four anthropomorphic winged beings all leaning in different directions with the sun directly overhead.

"I've got to have LJ look at this." She stepped down from her stool and began walking rapidly toward LJ's office.

After entering the room and making the turn that would take her to LJ's desk, she said, "LJ, come see what I…." before stopping in her tracks.

LJ and Max Dylan were standing as close as two people could. There was an unmistakable look of guilt on LJ's face, and Max looked like the cat that ate the canary.

Refusing to let either woman see her distress, Kylie schooled her features. "Sorry. I'll speak with you later." She turned and walked—she wanted to run—away as fast as she could.

†

LJ hadn't expected Max to show up since she'd made it perfectly clear she wanted nothing to do with her.

"LJ, darling, I need your help." Max breezed into her office and smiled before kissing her on the lips.

"Stop that. I told you to leave me alone."

Max gave her a pointed look. "Judging by those perky nipples, I'd say you're glad to see me."

LJ threw her arms across her chest. She'd been thinking about Kylie, and that always made her nipples harden. "Get out."

"I've just been speaking with Rob about some of my

students coming here for a lesson in reconstruction. I doubt he'd be happy to hear you refused to discuss it with me."

"You can send me an email with the criteria, and I will set up a time." LJ gave Max her best glare. "Now leave."

Max moved closer and grinned. "You know as well as I do that you don't mean that."

LJ grabbed her wrist and twisted it. "Oh, I mean every word. Now get out."

"Hmm, I love it when you get physical." Max traced a finger down LJ's cheek. "Are you as turned on as I am?" she whispered.

When she heard Kylie's voice, LJ snapped her head in that direction. She saw a mixture of horror, sadness, and disappointment in Kylie's eyes. "Kylie, wait," she said as Kylie left.

Kylie kept on walking.

LJ made a move to follow, only to have Max grab her arm. "Your little friend can wait. I can't." She pulled LJ to her and kissed her hard.

After wrestling herself free from Max's hold, LJ slapped her face. "Get out and don't come back unless you want to have all relations with the museum severed."

"You can't do that. I'm too important."

"Are you sure about that? Go ahead and try it and see how it works out for you, Max."

She grinned. "You've got a thing for your little helper, don't you?"

"Get out," LJ snarled.

"Oh, I bet Rob would like to know that little tidbit."

"Go for it, Max. See where it gets you." LJ shoved past her. "Don't be here when I get back."

†

"What a fool I've been." Kylie stood sobbing in a corner by the door of the workroom. "How can I ever compete with someone like that? No wonder she doesn't want me when she can have that."

"You don't have to compete with anyone, Kylie. You're the only one I see."

Kylie shook LJ's hand off her shoulder. "I know what I saw."

"You saw a woman who arrived, uninvited I might add, and who doesn't seem to know what the word *no* means."

"There wasn't enough room between the two of you for air."

LJ took her shoulders and turned her. "Kiley, there is nothing going on between Max and myself. Yes, she'd like there to be, but I'm not interested."

"Why don't you want me?" Kylie tired but failed at keeping her tears from falling. "I thought we were getting close," she whispered.

"We are."

When LJ lifted her chin and kissed her, Kylie's anger and sorrow melted and desire took its place. She leaned into the kiss as it intensified. For a moment, she forgot where they were. She wanted nothing more than to feel LJ's body close to hers. The banging of a distant door brought them out of their reverie.

"I guess this isn't where we should be doing this."

LJ smiled. "Tonight…I know it is not our usual night, but do you think we can have some alone time?"

Kylie put her head on LJ's shoulder. "Yes, if you can wait until after Ryan goes to sleep."

"You're going to make me wait that long?" LJ teased.

"Remember, waiting is a virtue."

"I'm tired of being virtuous." LJ grinned and ran a finger down Kylie's cheek. "So what is it you came to tell me?"

Kylie grabbed LJ's hand. "I think I've found a clue to the glyph."

After increasing the magnification, LJ began looking intently at what Kylie had pieced together. "I've never seen anything like this."

"Do you think it's the key to the mystery?"

"Perhaps. It's a picture on some form of pottery of that depicts these winged beings. I'm not sure of the significance. Maybe it's some sort of clock or season indicator." LJ pointed to the artifact. "It looks like there should be more to it."

"Yes. I saw that, but there aren't any more pieces."

"Let's look around the same area and see what else turns up."

For the rest of the day, LJ worked by Kylie's side as they tried to discover more of the puzzle.

†

LJ held Kylie's hand as they walked down the stairs after tucking Ryan in.

"Mommy."

"Good night, Ryan."

"Mommy, I want to tell you something."

"What?"

"I love you."

Kylie smiled. "I love you too, now go to sleep."

"I love you, Lgie."

LJ stopped and gave Kylie a quizzical look. "Do you think she means it?"

"Of course. She wouldn't have said it if she didn't mean it."

"I love you too, Ryan."

They continued down the stairs and went into the kitchen.

"Want some coffee?" Kylie asked.

"No. I don't think so."

"How about some cookies and milk?"

LJ smiled. "I haven't had that in ages."

Kylie pulled a plate out of the cupboard. "Here, put some cookies on this and take it into the family room. I'll get the milk."

After placing the plate on the coffee table, LJ sat on the couch and smiled when Kylie came in carrying two glasses of milk.

"My gran used to tell me the only way to eat a cookie properly was to dunk it in milk. Do you mind?"

"Not at all. I happen to agree with her." Kylie took a cookie, broke it in half, dunked it in the milk glass, and then moved it to LJ's mouth.

"Mmmm, that is delicious."

"Tell me about your grandmother."

LJ leaned back, knowing it was time to confess all to Kylie. "When I was sixteen, my parents disowned me," she whispered.

"Why?"

LJ let out a derisive laugh. "I mistakenly thought they loved me and would support me in what I chose to do."

"They didn't want you to be an archaeologist?"

"No. It was because I chose to love Holly."

"Oh, LJ, that is horrible. I can't imagine turning my back on Ryan for any reason."

"You never know. We all have lines we refuse to cross. What do you think will happen if you told your parents about your feelings for me?"

"They will welcome you into the family. Of that I am certain."

"Are you? I was sure my parents would welcome Holly." A sad expression filled LJ's face. She snickered. "At that age I was stubborn and was going to prove to them that they couldn't run my life. In the end, they walked away and I showed them nothing."

"Do you have any brothers or sisters that supported you?"

"I have two brothers, but I haven't heard from them"—she shrugged—"since it happened."

"Have you tried to contact them?"

LJ shook her head. "They are both younger than me, and I'm sure my parents made sure they too thought I was a deviant. Why would I want to subject myself to their contempt of my sexuality too?"

"You don't know that though, do you?"

"No, and I'm not going to find out."

"What about grandparents?"

"There was only Gran. She didn't judge me. In fact, she went to my parents to try to persuade them to change their minds. When they refused, she had all my things packed up and taken to her home. She gave me a room and a place to stay when school was out."

"She sounds wonderful."

"She was." LJ took another bite of a cookie. "She was the only one to support me and welcomed Holly."

Kylie pulled her into a hug and kissed her softly on

the cheek. "I wish I could explain why that happened to you, but I can't. I don't understand how a parent can throw a child away. Just know that I am here for you always. Never doubt that."

Kylie could feel LJ's pain and desperately wanted to make it go away but knew that was impossible.

"I won't." LJ moved away. "I better get going."

"Are you sure?"

"Yes."

Kylie frowned. They had come so far, yet LJ still balked at going further in their relationship. "Then I will wait until the time is right."

"Hey, what do you say we take a trip some weekend out to my ranch? I bet Ryan will love riding the horses."

Kylie's eyes widened. "You have a ranch?"

"Yes. My gran left it to me."

"I know Ryan would love that. Hell, I would love that."

"Great. Let me know which weekend is good for you and I'll call Ben and make sure everything is in order."

"The weekend after next is good. My folks have been so busy this last month with their new RV that we haven't spent much time with them. They're going to visit friends in Wyoming next week, and they wanted us to stop by this weekend." Kylie grinned. "You can come with us."

"Not yet." LJ moved toward the door. "I think I'll stop by the museum on my way home and take another look at what you found today."

Kylie looked at her watch. "It's a little late for that. Why not look again in the morning after a good night's sleep?" She shook her head. "Okay, I know better than to think you're going to do that. Just promise me you won't spend the night there."

"I won't."

"Will you come to dinner tomorrow night? Ryan always asks me every morning when Lgie is coming back."

"After being a fixture in your home four times a week, I'd think the novelty would have worn off by now."

Kylie laughed. "That Barbie mansion you bought her sealed the deal. You're her best friend for life."

"I like her too. Unfortunately, I have that fundraiser tomorrow night, and if I want to get more funding so I can go back to Peru, I have to go."

"Oh yeah I forgot about that." Kylie smiled.

"Why don't you come with me?"

"I don't know. I'd feel out of place."

"Hey, I went out with you and your friends."

"You got me there. Let me see if I can get my folks to come here and stay with Ryan."

"Sounds good to me. We won't have far to go since it's at the museum. It starts at seven and we don't have to stay long...I never do and everyone knows that." LJ pulled Kylie to her and kissed her lips.

"Mmmm, sure you won't stay?"

"Yes."

"Have you ever taken a date to a fundraiser before?"

"No. You're the first."

"Good, I like the sound of that."

LJ gave her another quick kiss. "I'll see you in the morning."

"Yes, you will. Don't stay up too late."

LJ grinned. "I'll try not to."

†

Kylie's parents couldn't babysit, so she arranged for a neighbor girl to stay with Ryan while she went to the fundraiser with LJ. She'd hurried home after work to get Ryan situated and get ready. Now she was standing in the atrium of the museum with a glass of wine in hand, waiting for LJ to arrive.

"Kylie, what a pleasant surprise. I didn't know you were coming tonight."

"LJ invited me." Kylie looked at Rob's face and saw surprise there.

"That's a first. She's never come with anyone. Where is she?"

"She hasn't arrived yet, which is good because I'd like to speak to you about how to go about being a sponsor for her next dig."

Rob's eyes widened. "Are you serious?"

"Absolutely. After working on the reconstructions, I see how important what she's doing is, and I'd like to see what it would take to fund some of the dig." Kylie looked around the room. "That is why everyone is here, isn't it?"

"If you'll come by my office tomorrow, I'll give you a packet about donations to the museum."

"I don't think you understand. Any funding I give must go to the dig in Peru only."

"That can be arranged."

"What can be arranged?" LJ asked.

A warm glow spread throughout Kylie. "Hi." She gave LJ a slight hug.

"Hi. Sorry I'm late."

"You're not. I was early." Kylie looked at Rob. "We were just discussing the funding for your dig. I see many people I haven't seen since Ted died, and I know they all have deep pockets."

"If you two will excuse me, I need to circulate." Rob patted Kylie's arm. "I'm glad you are here."

When LJ walked into the room and saw Kylie, she had to catch her breath. The black dress that clung to every curve of her body made LJ's own body react pleasurably. She was a bit concerned when Kylie hugged her, even though it was brief. The look on Rob's face as he watched the action was a mixture of curiosity and surprise.

"You shouldn't have hugged me."

"Why? This is a date, isn't it?"

"Yes, but...."

"No buts." Kylie took her hand. "Come on. I see they have hors d'oeuvres and I'm starving."

"Are you sure you want to hold my hand?"

Kylie smiled. "That's what I do when I'm on a date. Any objections?"

"No, but what about all those people who knew you when you were married?"

"What about them?"

"They'll talk about you being with me. And I'm sure there is some sort of policy that prohibits us from working together and dating."

Kylie snorted. "Let them think and say what they want, I don't care. Ryan, you, my parents, my granny, and my friends know how I feel, and they are okay with it. The others are irrelevant. As for the museum, if they give us trouble we'll fight it. Besides, I bet they're all jealous because I'm here with a beautiful woman and they aren't."

"Your granny knows?"

"Yes. She was my sounding board early on. You

should meet her. I think the two of you would get along just fine."

LJ squeezed her hand. "Come on, the hors d'oeuvres await you. After that, I'll have to speak to some of these people." LJ shrugged. "If I want funding I have to socialize."

Chapter Seventeen

That Friday, Ryan's grandparents had picked her up from school. Virginia, who was preparing dinner, smiled at Ryan, who was sitting at the kitchen table coloring.

"It seems like ages since I've seen you." Virginia hugged her granddaughter. "I wish you and your mommy could go on the trip with us."

"Mommy said that maybe in the summer we can go with you."

"I'd like that." Virginia knew she and Carl had spent so much time planning the trip in their new RV that they'd neglected Kylie and Ryan. It had been a few weeks since she'd spent significant time with her granddaughter. "I've missed you. Tell me what you've been doing?"

"I've been playing with Lgie." The answer was casual.

"Who is Lgie, Ryan? I don't recall that name from your school list."

"Lgie is my new friend, and she plays with me."

Ryan looked up from her coloring and smiled.

"Is she new to your class at school, honey? I will have to add her to the list."

"No, she comes to my house and we play, then she talks to Mommy after I go to bed," Ryan continued, concentrating on her coloring before looking up at her grandmother. "Mommy thinks she is her friend, but she really is mine."

Virginia gave Ryan a curious look. "Really? She's your friend but stays and talks to your mommy?"

Ryan smiled. "Yes. Please don't tell mommy she's really my friend. It would hurt her feelings."

Virginia patted her granddaughter on the head. "Don't worry, I won't tell her."

"Mommy doesn't cry anymore." Ryan went back to what she'd been doing.

"Your mommy was crying?" *I can't believe I spent so much time on the RV that I missed that my daughter was crying.*

"Lgie makes her laugh and smile. I like that better than crying."

"I would too." Virginia couldn't help her frown as she tried to get her head around who Lgie was and what her relationship with Kylie was. Virginia had attributed her and Carl's involvement in planning their upcoming trip and Kylie's new job as the reason they hadn't seen as much of each other recently. Perhaps this Lgie person was also keeping her busy.

The front door opened, and Kylie came inside smiling. *Now I can get some answers.*

"I'm finally here. Sorry I took so long." Kylie breezed into the room, kissed her mother's cheek, and patted Ryan on the head.

207

"Not a problem." Virginia smiled. "Ryan, will you go find Grandpa and tell him your mommy is here?" She smiled at Kylie. "I hope you're hungry. I made your favorite."

"We can't stay for dinner."

"Please, Mommy," Ryan pleaded.

"No."

"We haven't seen you much lately, and I was hoping we could visit over dinner."

"We're going to spend the weekend with you."

After Ryan left in search of her other favorite playmate, Virginia cleared her throat. "Ryan tells me someone named Lgie is her new friend. Is she a new girl at school?"

Kylie shook her head and sucked in a breath. "I see Ryan has been talking about her new playmate." A small, nervous laugh escaped as she sat down.

"So she *is* Ryan's friend. Is she imaginary? She told me you and Lgie spend time together after she goes to bed."

Imaginary? God, I hope not. "She's my friend that Ryan has fun playing with."

"How old is she?"

"My age." Kylie worked at keeping her voice steady so as not to show her nervousness. "Mom, when Daddy gets here, I would like to speak with you both about something."

"I found him, here he is." Ryan was exuberantly dragging her grandfather into the room.

Carl gave his daughter a kiss. "Hi, sweetheart. I hope you two can stay for dinner so we can tell you about our upcoming trip."

"I'm afraid not, Daddy. We can catch up on that when you come to my house tomorrow. Right now I'd like to talk with you and Mom about something." She looked at them expectantly. "If you have the time." Kylie's resolve was slipping away, and doubt began muddling her brain. *They're great parents, and just because LJ's parents reacted as they did doesn't mean they will. Right?*

"I'll listen while I finish up dinner," Virginia said.

"Okay. What's up?" Carl smiled and patted his wife's back.

Kylie motioned for Ryan to come to her. She bent over and whispered, "Go out to the car and tell Lgie to come on inside." She then gave her a big hug and kiss.

"Okay, Mommy." Ryan turned away and headed for the front door.

"Where is she going?" Virginia asked.

"I need her to get something out of the car for me." Kylie sucked in another breath. "There's something I need to tell you both. Please understand I'm not asking for your blessing or permission. I just want to be honest and up front with you."

"This all sounds very mysterious. Should I be worried? There is something different about you, Kylie. *Glow* is the only word I can think of." Carl smiled at his daughter. "You look positively radiant."

"Does this have to do with Lgie?"

"Who's Lgie?" Carl asked.

Kylie looked at her mother. *Nothing ever escapes her.* In that moment Kylie recognized that her mother probably knew the significance of what she was going to say.

"You've found someone you care about, haven't you?" Virginia was grinning.

"Does it show?" She looked at her mother.

"Yes, it does, darling. Are you happy?"

Kylie could feel a smile crossing her face as a vision

of LJ came to her mind. She looked at her parents and knew the rightness of what she was about to tell them. "I never knew what happiness was until now. I want you to meet LJ—"

"LJ? As in Dr. LJ Evans?"

Kylie shrank back slightly at Carl's intense gaze.

"Isn't Dr. Evans a woman?" He glared at her. "Are you telling us you are in love with a woman?"

"There's nothing wrong with that," Kylie countered. She gave her mother a fervent look.

"I think not, young lady!" Carl bellowed.

Virginia took her husband's hand. "Look at her, Carl. Have you ever seen her happier? I know I haven't."

"Happiness has nothing to do with it, Ginny. She will not be in an unnatural relationship." His face turned red. "You will not see this woman again. Do you hear me?"

Virginia glared at her husband and squeezed his hand hard. "Now you listen to me, Carl Aldridge, our daughter is happy, and that fact alone is all that matters to me. The way I see it, she is an adult and can do whatever she wants. Now, we shall welcome LJ into our family as if she were our own. Is that understood?"

Kylie didn't recall ever hearing her mother raise her voice to her father in such a way. It was clear from her tone that there would be no argument. Despite her father's words, Kylie had a sense of peace that she knew would carry her forward.

"Is that where Ryan went?" Virginia asked.

Kylie nodded. "Yes. They should be here in a few minutes. This isn't how I planned on telling you. I was hoping tomorrow at dinner you would meet her and get to know her then."

Carl grumbled, "I won't be attending."

"Stop that at once." Virginia thumped him on the arm. "*We* will be there."

LJ was waiting in the car listening to music when a tap on the window surprised her. She hadn't seen anyone come out of the house. She pressed a button and lowered the window.

"Mommy told me to get you and bring you inside," Ryan said.

"This isn't supposed to happen until I'm ready to meet them," LJ whispered. "Ryan, can you tell your mommy I'll wait here for her?"

"Lgie, come on. Grammie and Grandad are waiting for us."

LJ looked at Ryan, who was giving her the puppy-dog look that always got her what she wanted. She opened the door and took Ryan's hand. "Okay. Let's go."

When they entered the house, she heard the voice of a woman who sounded as though she was reaming someone out. A chill ran down her spine as she knew history was going to repeat itself.

She let Ryan, who was holding her hand, drag her into the kitchen, where she saw a woman who was smiling in her direction and a very angry-looking man.

"Here she is, Mommy." Ryan beamed. "Grammie and Granddad, this is my best friend, Lgie."

LJ tried but could feel that she was failing miserably at hiding her apprehension.

Kylie's mother walked up to her and embraced her. "Virginia Aldridge." She held out her hand. "Welcome to our home. Have a seat and tell us all about yourself. I hope you'll be staying for dinner. I have plenty."

After looking at Kylie, who gave her a smile and a nod, LJ's shoulders relaxed as a warm feeling of love filled her heart. She wasn't so sure about the father, but Kylie's mother had welcomed her into their family without recrimination.

"Thank you. I'm not sure about dinner. That will be up to Kylie." LJ paused for a moment as she searched for the right words. "I'm at a loss, and I don't know what to say. My own family was never this kind to me." She shrugged. "They disowned me."

Virginia took her by the arm and pointed to one of the kitchen table chairs. "Sit." She looked at Kylie. "There is no better way to get to know a person than over a home-cooked meal. That way I can find out all about you, LJ."

Kylie and Ryan followed suit and sat at the table on either side of LJ. LJ gave Kylie a questioning look.

"I was going to introduce you when you were ready," Kylie whispered. "Ryan beat me to it."

LJ nodded and grinned before looking back at Kylie's father, who stood scowling with his arms folded. He was obviously not happy about the situation.

"Carl Aldridge." He didn't offer his hand. "Welcome to our home, LJ," he ground out. His words sounded forced and cold but he was at least making the effort, which was more than her father did. "Hey, Ryan, what do you say you come help me outside in the garden until it's suppertime? I saw a bunny out there this morning." Carl held out his hand to Ryan.

"A bunny! Let's go." Ryan grabbed her grandfather's hand.

Carl grinned before looking at the women. "If you will excuse us. Text me when dinner is ready."

Virginia watched as her husband and granddaughter

went out of the room. "Give him time, he'll come around."

"From your lips to God's ears," Kylie said.

"So, LJ, or shall I call you Lgie?"

For the first time since she'd entered the home, LJ smiled. "LJ is good."

†

Dinner was finished, and Ryan and LJ excused themselves to the family room to color. Carl, who was sitting in his chair, glared at her.

LJ looked around the well-decorated room. The soft, tan walls complemented the dark leather sectional and the Mission-style furnishings. A huge flat-screen television was across one wall, and a bookcase was along another. "Mr. Aldridge, I was noticing your arrowhead collection in the bookcase. Did you find them around here?"

Carl looked at her in surprise. "Why, yes. I found them south of here when I was a kid."

"Do you mind if I take a look at them?"

"Go ahead."

By the tone of the man's voice, LJ knew he was only making an effort to please his wife who had just entered the room. Although he told her it was okay to touch his artifacts she knew he didn't mean what he said.

She carefully looked at the assortment. "Wow, I can't believe it! You actually have a bird arrowhead. You generally don't see many of them." She pointed to another one. "This one is pre-Columbian, isn't it?"

Carl got up and went over to where LJ was standing. "That one is my pride and joy. When I found it, I took it to the university museum for them to look at. They wanted me to donate it...I was twelve at the time and told them no." His

213

voice had softened and he picked up a spearhead. "What do you make of this one?"

LJ took the artifact and turned it over several times before giving the man a thoughtful look. "It's definitely native to this part of the country. If you look here"—she pointed to the base—"it is completely tooled. The surprising thing is its size. We don't usually see them this big. Hmm, I think this is a rare find."

"Yeah, that is what I thought too. You just don't find anything like this anymore. As a boy, I remember finding them all the time along with fossils in rocks. Now, there is nothing to be found."

"You know, Mr. Aldridge, I have a ranch about twenty miles outside of town. You are welcome to come out there and look for both fossils and arrowheads. My caretaker tells me he finds arrowheads all the time when he's plowing." LJ gave him her most engaging smile. "One time he even came across a grinding stone and the rock used with it."

Carl was warming to the woman. She wasn't much of a conversationalist, but if the way she looked at Kylie was any indication, she truly cared for his daughter. His collection of arrowheads was a prized possession, and her interest in it was a plus in his estimation.

"Some of the fondest memories I have are going out with my dad looking for arrowheads and other artifacts. When Kylie took archaeology courses in college, I hoped that one day she and I could carry on that tradition."

"And did you?" LJ asked.

"Once or twice." He shrugged. "Ted took up most of her free time." He eyed LJ. "I guess now that it looks like

Kylie wants you to be part of the family, you should know I never liked the guy." He carefully appraised the woman standing next to him. "I will hold you to the same standard I held him. I hope you don't disappoint me like he did." He watched as LJ looked at Kylie.

"I will never treat her with anything but respect."

"I believe you. Just know I will be keeping my eye on you." Carl fixed her with a glare. "Both Kylie and Ryan are the world to me, and I don't take kindly to someone hurting them."

"I have no intention of doing that, sir."

"It will take me a while to get used to this relationship between you and my daughter." He paused and cleared his throat. "But I can see how happy she is, and I promised my wife I'd give it a go, and that's what I'll do."

"I appreciate that, sir."

Carl regarded her for a moment longer. "If you give me the directions to your ranch, I would like to check those arrowheads out."

"Sure thing. Do you have a map? I can show you where my place is, and I'll draw you a map of the ranch showing where the best dig areas are located."

Carl put a tentative arm around her shoulder. "That's what I like, someone who knows the value of a map. Come on into my study. Do you want a beer?"

"Sure, that sounds good." A smiling LJ followed him into his study.

Chapter Eighteen

The front door jerked open and Ryan squealed, "Lgie," and flung herself at the woman.

LJ swung Ryan into her arms and kissed her cheek. "Hi, are you ready to go?"

Ryan wrapped her arms around LJ's neck and hugged her. "I love you, Lgie. I can't wait to see the horses."

"Did you pack Barbie?"

"Oh yes. Mommy bought her an outfit for riding horses."

LJ looked up and caught Kylie's gaze. She was standing in the hallway wearing a goofy grin. "Good morning." She gently put Ryan down before walking toward Kylie and wrapping her in a warm embrace. "How's my girl doing today?" she whispered.

Kylie snuggled closer, and LJ could feel every inch of her.

"Wonderful, now that you're here."

An insistent tug on her jeans made LJ look down.

"May I help you?" She released Kylie and squatted to Ryan's level.

"When are we going to see the horses, Lgie? You promised I could ride one."

LJ chuckled and looked at Kylie's feet. "And you will. Right now we need to see if we can find your mom's shoes since she can't ride a horse in bare feet."

Kylie was laughing. "I seem to have a problem with that. I can't find them anywhere. Ryan, will you run upstairs and look for me?"

Ryan held up one finger. "Wait right her for me, k?"

LJ let her gaze drift to Kylie. "I'm not going anywhere. I'll be right here when you find her shoes."

Ryan took off running, and LJ stood before embracing Kylie again. "Did you really lose your shoes?"

"No. I wanted to kiss you." She licked her lips before kissing LJ.

"Mommy," Ryan said, bounding down the stairs, "I can't find them."

Kylie pulled back but kept her arms around LJ. "Will you look in the family room and the kitchen, please?"

"Okay."

"I know I saw you last night, but I've missed you," LJ said before kissing Kylie's waiting lips.

"Mmmm, how did you sleep last night?" Kylie kissed her again.

The kiss began to intensify just as Ryan came back into the hall. "Mommy, I have your shoes. Can we see the horses now?"

The embrace ended, and LJ gave Kylie a wink and a smile. "We'll finish this later."

"Yeah, yeah, yeah…promises, promises." Kylie patted LJ's backside. "Our suitcases are by the door."

Once everything was loaded into LJ's truck, they headed west toward their weekend getaway.

†

Every time LJ opened the gate before driving down the long dirt road to Rhodes End, her thousand-acre ranch, LJ would recall the small, sweet woman who always loved her no matter what. Her gran had been her rock, and losing her was the greatest loss of her life.

The main house was painted white with green shutters and had a dark green metal roof. The front porch had a swing and several rocking chairs that had seen many days of use over the last fifty years. Off to one side were two additional houses and several smaller buildings. As with all ranches, the obligatory rusty old car and tractor sat inside the fence along with the newer equipment. Behind the main house stood a huge barn also painted white and green. Trees dotted the area, along with a beautiful flower garden.

"Oh, LJ, this place is wonderful!" Kylie exclaimed as she got out of the truck. "That barn is magnificent. Can we go inside?" She had a look of awe on her face.

"Where are the horses, Lgie? Where are they?" Ryan squealed.

Warmth coursed through LJ's body as she stood on her property holding the hand of the delightful child who had won her heart. Her eyes drifted to Kylie, and her heart filled with happiness in what she knew was love.

"Tell you what"—LJ squatted in front of Ryan— "why don't you and your mom look around for a little bit while I talk to Ben over there?" She pointed to a man standing nearby. "Then we can go see the horses."

Ryan gave LJ a gigantic hug that almost knocked her

218

to the ground. "Whoa, that was some hug." Ben Morgan, the caretaker, was coming her way, and she stood. "Go on now, Ryan. I'll be right back."

Ryan ran with delight to her mother and jumped up and down while talking animatedly. LJ was smiling when she met Ben. "Hi, is the house ready?" The smile left her face, and the cool, hard exterior that only came down for the two Wilcox girls appeared.

"Yep, everything is in order. I need to go into town for feed and won't be back 'til late. Is there anything else you need before I go?"

To LJ the man looked much younger than his sixty-two years. He had been with LJ's grandmother for as long as she could remember and had agreed to stay on as caretaker after her death. She knew he loved Rhodes End and had treated the place with the respect and care it deserved. For that, LJ was eternally grateful.

"Yes, can you take the suitcases out of the truck and put them in the house for me while I show my guests around?" She made sure that although tone of her voice was cool, it was respectful.

"Sure will, missy."

"Thanks." She turned only to come back around. "Ben, which pasture do you think the horses are in?"

"I saw them up on the north ridge earlier this mornin'." He lifted two suitcases out of the truck.

"Great, thanks, see you later." Then she strode toward the barn and her two ladies.

Ben watched her go. He still remembered her as a strange child who would rather dig in the dirt than play with the other kids. In a way, he had always felt an affinity for her since he also loved the land.

When her grandmother passed away, he saw the devastation on LJ's face and gladly agreed to stay on and take care of Rhodes End. He never knew the entire story of how the young woman came to own the property but suspected it had something to do with her family. They had stopped visiting the farm after LJ came to live at the ranch.

She had always been fair and generous with him, allowing him a substantial salary and to share in the revenues from the sale of wheat and cows. Over the years since Marion Rhodes's death, her granddaughter visited monthly but had never brought anyone with her until now. He was glad to see her here with someone for his heart always went out to the sad, lonely woman.

"Best get myself to town and stop burnin' daylight."

†

"Lgie, Lgie, where are the horses?" Ryan asked excitedly.

"Keep your eyes open. We should be seeing them anytime now."

Driving over the rough terrain was an adventure in itself. The three passengers of the truck bounced up and down, looking somewhat like school kids on a bus with each rut they crossed.

Ryan was laughing and babbling to anyone who would listen. As they neared the ridge, five or so horses came into view. "Lgie, there they are! The horses, we've found the horses," she screamed.

LJ couldn't help but laugh. Ryan's unabashed enthusiasm for the wonders of life touched her heart in a way she'd never expected it to.

"I think you've scored more points with her." Kylie rested a hand on LJ's thigh. "As if you need any more."

"I'll take all I can get from you both."

"Well, you know what you have to do to score the big points with me." Kylie squeezed LJ's thigh before wiggling her eyebrows.

"Just how many points are we talking about?"

"Lgie, let's get closer," Ryan squealed.

LJ looked at the horses as the truck closed in on them. They all lifted their heads in its direction before immediately going back to chomping on the grass. They were obviously unimpressed. She stopped the truck, and the horses continued to ignore them. "Roll down your window, and I will call them over, and then we can give them treats," LJ said.

After a series of whistles, three of the horses came toward the truck.

Ryan scrambled over her mother to get to the open window.

"Ryan, let you mother go first." LJ handed Kylie a treat. "Lean across Ryan and hold the treat flat in your hand. Otherwise they will think your fingers are treats too." She laughed at the look of horror that crossed Kylie's face.

"You're kidding, right?"

"Nope, afraid not. Just put it in your palm and they'll take it."

Cautiously Kylie held her hand out the window as the first horse, a pinto, came up to the truck. He pressed his lips against Kylie's palm and took the treat. "That felt so weird."

Ryan grabbed a treat and pushed her mother's hand out of the way before holding her hand out the window.

"Keep it flat," Kylie cautioned.

"Here, horsey. I have a treat too." She held it out, and

a big black mare took it.

Soon all five horses were moving around the truck in search of treats. The windshield had horse lip prints all over it, and two of them were attempting to move their heads completely inside the truck. Ryan, Kylie, and LJ were all laughing at the horses' antics.

"LJ, it is getting a bit cramped in here," Kylie said, laughing. "I never realized how big their heads were until they were up close and personal." She continued to laugh as she tried desperately to get the horse to back out of the truck. "Help me get this one out of here. I think Ryan is pinned to the seat."

Ryan was shrieking with delight, her eyes flashing as she petted the horses while continuing to give them treats.

LJ watched as her favorite horse—a paint—leaning into the rider's seat. "We should have brought a camera. No one would believe this." As soon as she started the truck, the horses withdrew and moved slowly away. Ryan still held her hand out the window.

"Ryan, no more treats. We need to get going," Kylie told her.

"But Lgie, can't we stay longer? Pleeease."

She is so cute when she makes that pitiful face. "Not right now. I'll bring you back out in the morning. Maybe we can take a ride on one of the horses. Would you like that?"

"Oh yes. Can we really do that?" Her eyes widened.

"Yes, really." LJ couldn't help but smile.

"What about me?" Kylie protested.

"Well"—LJ winked—"what do you think, Ryan? Should we let your mom come back with us in the morning?"

"Only if she sits in the middle."

Both women smiled and said in unison, "I can deal with that."

†

"LJ, can we look at that amazing barn now?" Kylie asked when they returned from seeing the horses.

"What's the big deal? It's just barn." LJ grinned and wrapped her arm around Kylie's waist. "Let's go. I think you'll be fascinated by what's inside."

"What do you mean?"

"You'll see." LJ took Ryan's hand. "I think there might be some horses in there too."

Ryan squealed with delight. "Can we see them?"

"Yes, come with me."

The doors swung open, and Kylie held her hand to her mouth. The interior of the barn was massive. On one side were ten stalls all with fresh hay, and four of them were occupied. On the other side, several neat rows of antiques occupied four walled-off areas.

"Was this all your grandmother's?" Kylie walked over to the first area and ran a finger over a cherry hutch. She looked at LJ and saw her pained expression. "You loved her very much, didn't you?"

"She was my world for such a long time." LJ looked away, and when she looked at Kylie again, she saw tears.

"Tell me."

"The real reason I don't come out her very often is that it's too painful." She swiped at her eyes. "God, what's wrong with me? I'm never this emotional."

Kylie rested her head on LJ's chest. "You have to let it all go. I don't think your grandmother would want this for you." She looked in LJ's eyes. "Is it?"

"When we were out there with Ryan and the horses, I could feel the happiness being here once gave me. For a moment my gran was there with us."

Kylie put her hand over LJ's heart. "That's because she is here and always has been. You just never let her out."

"It hurt too much."

"It doesn't have to. All you need to do is remember the good times and the love you have for her, and your heart will fill with happiness and warmth."

"I don't know how."

"I do."

"Will you help me?"

"Always. Don't you know that by now?"

"Lgie, look at me!"

Both women turned to see Ryan standing halfway up a stall railing holding on by one hand.

Looking terrified, LJ took off at a run and scooped Ryan up in her arms before she could fall. "You shouldn't do that. You could hurt yourself."

"I wanted to see the horses."

"Next time ask me and I'll help you." LJ hugged her close. "I don't know what I'd do if something happened to you," she whispered.

"I love you, Lgie."

"Me too. Please don't scare me like that again."

"You know better than to do that, young lady," Kylie said.

"I'm sorry, Mommy."

LJ cleared her throat. "What do you say we go in the house and see what there is for dinner?"

Kylie's stomach took that moment to growl, and she laughed. "Sounds like a good idea to me."

†

The inside of the main house was warm and cozy, and Kylie suspected it was just as LJ's grandmother had left it. An old, deep purple divan dominated the living room along with a piano. It also had a recliner, a well-worn, overstuffed chair with an ottoman, and walls filled with family pictures. The kitchen was old as well, with a beautiful, well-worn, round oak table, and against one wall was a wooden larder complete with flour and sugar bins.

"Wow, would you look at this kitchen. It is fantastic." Kylie turned in a circle as she took in everything. "I can tell there was a lot of love in here."

"Yeah, my gran loved to cook. I'd come home and she'd always have a custard pie for me. If I asked her why she made it, she'd say because she knew I'd like it."

"Did you?"

"Yes. It was my favorite. I could always count on her making all my favorites."

"Those are the memories you need to keep in your heart and let out when you're feeling down." Kylie tapped her heart. "Do you feel it?"

LJ smiled. "I do. Thank you for reminding me." She moved to the refrigerator and opened it. "Let's see what Nina left for us."

"Who's Nina?"

"Ben's wife. He manages the place for me and they live in the bigger of the houses across the way."

"So what do we have?" Kylie stood hip to hip with LJ before they began pulling the meal out of the refrigerator.

That night they dined on fried chicken, mashed potatoes, corn, and blueberry cobbler.

†

"I'm so happy you asked us to come here. This place is awesome." Kylie waved her hand around the front room.

"It is, isn't it? I've missed seeing that. Thank you."

"For what?"

"For coming into my life and helping me open my eyes to what is important." LJ hugged Kylie close. "Want to sit out on the porch with me?"

"Sure." Kylie smiled happily. "Let me check on Ryan first. I can't believe she fell asleep at dinner."

"That isn't surprising since she was all over the place today."

"Be right back."

A minute later, Kylie walked out onto the porch.

"Is she okay?" LJ asked.

"She's sleeping with a blissfully happy look on her face, and it's all thanks to you." Kylie smiled at LJ, who was sitting on the swing with a blanket in her lap.

"Come join me." She motioned Kylie over and took her hand when she sat down. "Closer, sit closer and we can share the blanket. It gets cold out here at night."

Kylie leaned her head on LJ's shoulder. "I love this place. It's so peaceful out here."

After smoothing the blanket out over them, LJ stretched her legs out and crossed them at the ankles. Then she took Kylie's hand again, brought it to her lips, and kissed it gently. "You know," she began, "I never thought it would be possible to feel again after my gran died. It was like the final blow for me. I didn't know if I could ever love again either, especially after losing Holly." She stopped speaking, and it seemed to Kylie as if LJ were in another place and time.

Kylie waited patiently, expecting the letdown she always knew LJ would give her. LJ had always said she might not be able to offer her what she needed and deserved. Now, here on this porch in the middle of nowhere, she would be given the "I just want to be friends" talk. The very thought sent shivers through her body and a great sense of sadness in her heart.

"Is it too cold out here for you?" LJ asked. She looked intently at Kylie. "What's the matter? You look like you're about to cry."

Kylie heard the compassion and concern behind LJ's words and turned her head away.

LJ took her chin and brought her back. "Please, tell me."

"You're about to give the 'I just want to be friends' talk, and it breaks my heart." Kylie couldn't stop the tears from brimming over and flowing down her cheeks.

LJ cocked her head and raised an eyebrow. "That's news to me. Why would you think such a thing?"

Kylie took a deep breath. "You were talking about Holly and how you didn't think you could ever feel like that again. It only stands to reason there isn't room in your heart for anyone else." She lowered her head.

"You know what, Kylie Wilcox? You are a silly goose who jumps to conclusions."

Kylie's head snapped up, and she looked at LJ in puzzlement. "Then why were you waxing on so nostalgically?"

"If you remember, I mentioned my gran first. Yes, Holly left a hole in my heart, but it was nothing like the crater losing my gran left." LJ kissed her. "A part of me will always remember Holly and what we shared. I know now that she was my first love, and it was all-consuming at the time but...." LJ lifted her eyes to look into Kylie's face. "I was going to say I never considered the possibility of caring about someone else until you came into my life and that all changed."

"My heart aches for you when you're away, and it soars to the heavens when you are near," Kylie whispered.

The kisses began small, then erupted into a passion that astounded Kylie. She wanted and needed more as her body filled with electricity and desire. "Make love with me," she whispered.

"Are you sure that's what you want?"

"Yes. I've never been surer of anything in my life."

LJ knew that once they made love, there would be no turning back because she never wanted to be without Kylie in her life. Her parents were accepting of the possibility of them having a relationship, and for LJ that was important. They had held hands and kissed in public, and Kylie didn't flinch or turn away. It was finally time to take the next step.

LJ put an arm under Kylie's legs, lifted her off the swing, and carried her into the house. In the bedroom, she undressed Kylie, taking great care to be gentle and loving. For a moment, she stood looking at the naked body before her. Gazing into the gray eyes, she saw what she knew were love and desire. It was time to join the living and leave the relics behind.

Her passion increased after sliding naked next to Kylie before softly running her fingers over the trembling body. Soon she felt Kylie's fingers mirroring her movements. As she bent to kiss the waiting lips, LJ gloried in the absolute, overpowering desire and passion that filled her soul.

She lifted up and looked deep into Kylie's eyes, asking a silent question. Kylie smiled back and said yes with her eyes. With that, LJ took a hard, extended nipple in her mouth and began slowly sucking it while running her tongue over the surface.

Kylie responded with low moans as she caressed LJ's head, holding it in place.

When LJ lightly bit the nipple, Kylie's body exploded in a series of small, intense quivers. The only thing LJ cared about was making Kylie happy and showing her how much she cared for her. She moved to the other nipple as her hand stroked the inside of Kylie's trembling thighs. She nipped again at the bud of Kylie's nipple, making her body tremble.

Kylie grabbed her head and pulled her up for a kiss. It was so passionate and long that LJ found herself gasping for breath. Kylie was crying. "Have I hurt you?" she asked before kissing the tearstained cheeks.

"No," Kylie managed to say. "I have never felt like this before. It's so powerful. I want more, LJ. I want all you can give me."

Gently brushing blonde locks away, LJ smiled. "We have a lifetime." She kissed the waiting lips and she stroked Kylie's clitoris lightly. She was wet and ready, but LJ waited, taking her higher and higher. LJ's fingers slid inside easily, and Kylie instantly began moving.

LJ stopped her motion, gently kissing Kylie before guiding Kylie's hand down to her own saturated folds. For a moment, she closed her eyes and tried to control her overwhelming need and let her fingers moved through Kylie's wetness. Soon they were moving as one. They panted as they bore down on the other's fingers, wanting and needing release.

"Now, Kylie, now," LJ cried as one explosion of pleasure after another filled her.

Spent and lying in Kylie's arms, LJ went silent for a

time. She never thought she would be this unbelievably happy again. Yet, here she was in the arms of this wonderful woman. Most incredible of all was the unabashed love she felt for Kylie. It was astonishing how she hadn't seen how empty her life had been before Kylie came into it.

"It's amazing," Kylie said.

"What is?"

"For the first time in my life, I can relate to what all the love songs and poems mean. I never imagined my body would react in such a primal way." She ran a finger down LJ's chest. "Even more amazing is that my passion and desire is for you."

"Because I'm a woman?"

"No. You were so impossible when we first met that the thought of being here with you was the furthest thing from my mind. You're being a woman seems quite natural to me."

"I love you, Kylie. I think I always have. I just couldn't let myself believe it. I feel more passion and desire for you than I ever thought I would be capable of with anyone."

"Oh LJ, I love you so much."

Their kisses began once more, igniting their passion as their bodies again began to dance.

†

The next morning Kylie woke and frowned. LJ was gone, and all her insecurities and doubts resurfaced. *Was last night a one-night stand?* Then she heard laughter coming from outside the window. With a sheet wrapped around her naked body, Kylie walked to it and saw LJ pushing Ryan on a swing suspended from a very large oak. *How did I miss that?*

She opened the window. "Hey, I see you're getting your exercise early this morning."

LJ and Ryan looked at her. "Good morning, sleepyhead. Ryan and I thought we'd let you sleep in since you had such a late night." LJ winked.

"Mommy, Lgie is swinging me."

Kylie laughed. "You two be careful. I'll be right back I'm going to take a quick shower, then I'll make breakfast. What would you like?"

LJ gave her a knowing smile.

"I want pancakes," Ryan said.

"Okay, pancakes it is. As for you, Dr. Evans, I will fill your request later."

When the spray of the shower hit her body, Kylie was suddenly aware of how alive she felt. Her nipples were especially sensitive, and when she washed between her legs, she closed her eyes, recalling the night before. She wanted to be with LJ again and didn't see how that would be possible. *I'll just have to wait until we're alone tonight.*

†

LJ let Ryan go with Ben to the barn to feed the horses and headed for the kitchen, where she knew she'd find Kylie. She opened the door quietly and stood outside it for a moment, watching Kylie sway her hips in time with a song on the radio while she flipped pancakes. Then with sure steps, she moved behind her lover, wrapped her arms around her waist, and kissed her neck.

"Good morning."

"I heard you come in and hoped you'd come to me."

"Always."

"I wanted you when I woke up," Kylie whispered.

"Ryan knocked on the door and I heard her, so I told her to wait for me in her room and I'd be there in a minute."

Kylie turned around. "Oh. That was nice of you. Did she say anything about us sleeping together?"

"Not a word. It didn't seem to faze her. I got her dressed, and then we went outside."

"Where is she now?"

"Ben took her to the barn."

"How long do you think they'll be there?"

LJ's lips hoovered over Kylie's. "It usually takes him a half hour to forty-five minutes to feed the horses."

Kylie twirled around, took a pancake off the griddle, and turned off the burner before turning back to LJ. "I want to feel you inside me again."

LJ groaned. "Here?"

"No. I want you naked. Text Ben and tell him to let you know when he's bringing Ryan back."

LJ fumbled with her phone but managed to send the text while Kylie was leading her into the bedroom.

"Lock the door." Kylie began removing LJ's clothes.

†

After lunch, Kylie and LJ sat in the porch swing as they watched Ryan playing with her Barbie.

"I want to tell the world about us," Kylie said as they swung lightly. LJ's body stiffened. "Is something wrong?"

"I worry about the fallout once people know. I don't want you to have to experience what I did."

"You still don't get it, do you?"

"Apparently not."

"The people I care about and who genuinely love me

232

already know, and they accept us. The rest of them are unimportant to me."

"You haven't experienced what people can do and say. I couldn't bear to see you hurt in that way."

Kylie snuggled closer and kissed LJ's cheek. "I know what I feel and want, and I can handle anyone who has something negative to say about our relationship. You have to believe that."

LJ looked in Ryan's direction. "Look at her playing without a care in the world. Kids can be so cruel to each other. Do you really want to subject her to that?"

"That won't happen."

"It happens," LJ said in soft voice. "They won't be kind. I know; I've been there."

Kylie turned and took LJ by the shoulders. "Ryan is her own person and she loves us. I've taught her that love is above all else."

"But do you want to take the chance of her being a target of vicious people?"

"You still don't get it." Kylie shook her head. "I love you and I want you in my life forever. You and Ryan are my life, and I won't let anyone stand in my way, and that includes petty people." She kissed LJ. "You have to trust me on this."

"I do trust you. What do you say we take Ryan to see the horses one more time before we leave?"

"Sounds like a plan to me." Kylie stood and held out her hand. "There's one more thing."

"What's that?"

"Will you live with us?"

LJ snorted. "Can I have my own room?"

"You're kidding, right?"

A deep, rich laugh was her answer.

†

On the drive back to the city, Ryan laid on her head on her mother's lap and fell asleep. They had spent the rest of the day riding horses around the property, and the child was exhausted.

"I know your things aren't at the house yet, but will you stay with me tonight? I'll wash the clothes you have with you so you have something to wear to work tomorrow."

"Are you sure that's what you want?"

"Yes. I want to spend all my nights with you."

"What will you tell Ryan?" LJ glanced at her for a moment.

"That I love you and want to be with you." Kylie squeeze LJ's hand.

"It can't be as simple as that. Life has rules we all have to follow. I've found that most of those rules are complicated. That's what I was trying to tell you earlier this morning."

"And I was saying that love is simple unless we make it difficult," Kylie said. "What I feel for you is simple, and for me that's all that matters."

"Ryan knows we slept together at the ranch. Do you think she'll be okay with that when we get back at your house? I don't want to cause a problem. Maybe I should sneak out in the early morning?"

"There will be no sneaking around. I love you and am proud that you're a part of my life. If others don't like it, then that's their problem, not mine, and I hope not yours." She poked LJ in the arm. "Get it?"

"Yes. I never did like sneaking around." She looked at Kylie. "What about your folks? I think we should wait until they get back before I move in."

"Why? I don't need their approval, if that is what you're thinking."

"As a show of respect."

Kylie nodded. "Okay. I see your point, but I don't like it."

"They'll be back in ten days. I think we can hold out until then."

At a stop sign they kissed. "Hmm, I'm not so sure about that." Kylie leaned in for another kiss.

✝

On Monday morning, LJ went home for a change of clothing before going to the museum. She stood by the door to her office as she waited for Kylie to arrive. When she heard the familiar footsteps, she stepped out into the corridor and took Kylie by the hand, pulled her into her office, and closed the door. "I've missed you."

"I wanted you to stay and have breakfast with us this morning."

Their kiss was long, slow, and passionate, and LJ's heart hammered in her chest. "I don't know if I can wait until your parents get back from their trip to move in with you."

"Then don't."

"We never said anything to them about living together. What if they disapprove?"

"They won't, and if they do, I don't care. I want you in my life. To go to sleep with and wake up with in my arms."

"I like the sound of that."

"Is today too soon?" Kylie kissed her softly.

"Good thing I don't have much. Mostly clothes and

the rest; my books, I can bring next weekend."

"It's settled, then."

LJ nodded. "As much as I'd like to hide away with you in here all day, we need to do some work."

They left for the workroom and were soon busy reconstructing artifacts.

"Good, you're here," Rob said as he walked into the room. "LJ, I need to speak with you privately."

"Fine." LJ walked up to the man. "I'm really busy, so can we speak here?"

Rob nodded. "I've just come from a meeting with the board of regents about funding for a dig next summer."

"Did we get the money?"

"Yes, but there are conditions."

LJ looked at him suspiciously. "I will not compromise how I do things, and you know that."

"I do. Per their instructions, I have contacted Dr. Dylan and requested she supply us with three grad students to help in the reconstruction."

"No. Absolutely not. Kylie is the only one I trust to do the job."

"It was because of your new find last week that the funding was approved, but they want what your assistant is doing expedited, and the only way to accomplish that is to add more help."

LJ looked at Kylie to see if she was listening, but she seemed completely focused on what she was doing. "Kylie will be in charge." Rob raised his eyebrows. "I will not compromise on that point. She knows what she's doing, and I have no idea what kind of training the others will have."

"Are you saying Dr. Dylan hasn't given them proper instructions? She was at the dig with you last summer and has firsthand knowledge of the entire procedure."

"I didn't say that. All I'm saying is that Kylie will be in charge of the workroom and anyone who comes in here to help."

"Fair enough. You can expect them to be here this afternoon around one." Rob nodded and moved closer. "Can I take what I saw between you and Kylie at the fundraiser as an indication that you've let the past go?"

"Yes."

"Good. She's a keeper."

"She is that." LJ watched the curator leave before walking back to Kylie. "Did you hear that?"

Kylie smiled. "Yes. Does it mean that Dr. Dylan will be here too?"

"Don't know, don't care. If she or her students give you any trouble, I want to know about it immediately."

"Not to worry. You will be the first one I call before I deck the woman." Kylie laughed. "Just kidding."

"By the way...Rob approves."

Kylie scrunched her eyebrows together, then her eyes widened. "Of us?"

"Yes. He asked in so many words if we were a couple."

Kylie grinned. "See, people who truly care about us love us enough to let us find our own way."

Chapter Nineteen

The rest of the week went by smoothly. The grad students proved to have a solid base of knowledge for understanding what they were doing. Max Dylan had not appeared, and for that, LJ was grateful. She didn't want to fend the woman off.

Early one morning while Kylie and LJ were working with the artifacts, LJ let out a loud whoop. "Come see this. It's unbelievable."

Kylie hurried to her side and looked at the large plaque she had pieced together two weeks earlier. "You completed it." She looked around the table. "The first pieces were way over on the other side."

"I couldn't believe my eyes when I saw them."

"Do you know what it depicts?"

"When you first pieced it together, I thought it might be a depiction of the seasons, but now there are three more figures, so that can't be it."

"Maybe it's a way of telling time." Kylie's eyes

caught something in the corner of the newly added pieces. "Look at that there." She pointed to the top right corner. "If I didn't know better. I'd say it looks like a UFO."

LJ pulled the magnifying glass over the area and looked at it. "That's curious. It looks exactly like the Egyptian hieroglyphic for the letter *r*. But it can't be. This predates the Egyptians."

Kylie laughed. "So it could be a UFO, right?"

LJ shook her head and chuckled. "Sure, we can say that for now. This is another clue to discovering just who the people that inhabited the area were."

Kylie saw the look of wonderment on LJ's face and in her eyes. She was on the verge of a discovery that had the potential of redefining the Wari' peoples.

"Be right back. I'm expecting a picture that my colleague Jean Moreau in Paris sent me."

Kylie looked up to see LJ entering the room with a big smile on her face waving a sheet of paper. "What's up? Did you get the photograph?"

"Better than that." LJ held out the paper. "I submitted a paper on the artifacts and the new glyph we found to the archaeology society in Lima, Peru. This is the email Maricielo Castillo who is the curator of the National Museum of Archaeology in Lima, sent. Read what it says."

LJ,

Congratulations!

As you know every year we present an award to the individual we feel has done outstanding work in promoting Peruvian archaeology. Based on your superb insight into the Wari' tribe we are honored to recognize your achievements.

The event will be held at the museum on October 3, 2016 at 7:00 PM and we would be honored if you attended and gave a speech about your work and the theories that brought about your amazing discovery.
    Once again, congratulations,
Maricielo Castillo
National Museum of Archaeology *Curator*

"LJ, this is wonderful. You're going to accept aren't you?"
"Only if you will go with me."
"I wouldn't miss it."

†

    At last, she was living in the same home with Kylie and Ryan, and LJ was happier than she'd ever been. She adored Ryan and received high marks from the child in Barbie play. Often she would look up and see Kylie standing in the doorway with a goofy smile on her face.
    They had lived together for two weeks when Kylie's parents returned from their extended vacation to Wyoming. LJ wasn't happy about the prospect of telling Kylie's parents that they were living together. It was a clear indication that their relationship had taken the next step, and she didn't know how receptive they'd be. Telling Kylie's parents was a small price to pay for the joy of being with Kylie and Ryan. Everything she wanted or needed was in the house they now shared. When she was at home with Kylie and Ryan, she was filled with so much happiness that she couldn't keep from smiling.
    LJ looked over at Kylie, who was driving them home after work. "Are you sure about your folks coming for dinner

tomorrow?"

"Yes. My mom and dad have been back since last Sunday, and when I saw them last Tuesday I told them we'd gotten very close, and they didn't seem to have any problem with that."

"I'll go with your mom being okay with it, but I'm not so sure about your dad. I hope you're right."

"I am. Trust me on this." Kylie pulled her car into their driveway. "Hey, Ryan is with them, which means we've got the house to ourselves. Let's not waste the opportunity."

LJ sighed.

Kylie patted her hand. "Stop worrying. I have much more pleasurable things in mind."

"I like the sound of that." LJ finally let a smile curl her lips. "What are we waiting for?"

✝

"What time are they arriving?" LJ asked nervously.

"They should be here in about an hour and a half. When they get here, we can start the grill going for the steaks."

"Are you expecting me to cook the steaks? If you are, you are going to be very disappointed. I've never grilled anything in my life."

"You didn't have a way to cook at all the digs you've been to?"

"Sure we did, but I wasn't the one doing the cooking."

"For a big-time archaeologist, you certainly have led a sheltered life." Kylie laughed.

"No way. I just wasn't the cook. I can start fires and hack through dense jungles though, so if you need any of that, I'm your girl."

Kylie wrapped her arms around LJ. "You are my girl in all ways, whether you grill or not."

"Maybe we should just forget telling them that we are officially living together."

"Too late for that. I imagine Ryan has already let that cat out of the bag."

"Shit. I bet your dad is furious." LJ could feel her insides churning.

"Okay, yes, he was upset at first, but he's had two weeks to reconcile his feelings. All that time in the RV meant my mom had his undivided attention as she worked on his attitude." Kylie laughed. "Trust me, he didn't stand a chance. Now will you please lighten up?"

The door burst open, and Ryan came charging into the kitchen. "Lgie, look what Granddad and I made." She held out a ceramic dish filled with what looked like origami dragonflies. "He made them and I painted them."

LJ squatted down and looked at Ryan's treasures. "They are great. Did you thank your granddad for all his help?"

"Oh yes, but I did most of the work."

LJ looked up and winked at Carl. "That so? Well you two did a mighty fine job." She stood. "You're a good man to be so patient with her."

Carl nodded before walking over to Kylie. "What's for dinner?"

"Your favorite, Dad. Rib eye steaks, baked potato, beans, and a salad."

"She grillin' the steaks?" He pointed his thumb over his shoulder at LJ.

"No. That's always been your job. No one does it as good as you do."

LJ listened to the exchange and grinned. Kylie knew just how to play her father.

Kylie picked up the tray of steaks and headed out the patio door.

Carl turned and looked at her. "I went out to that ranch of yours last Wednesday. Nice spread you have there. Ben showed me around, and we found a few arrowheads."

"Did you bring them with you?"

Carl dug in his pocket and pulled out a piece of cloth. With great care, he unwrapped it. "Take a look."

With a big smile, LJ carefully took the cloth and looked at the three arrowheads. "The Tonkawa tribe originally inhabited this area before the Apache, then the Comanche pushed them out. My guess is that they are Comanche arrowheads. Those are what we usually find out at my place." She turned them over in her hand. "They are in very good condition and will be a great addition to your collection."

"That's what I thought." Carl patted her on the back. "I hope I can go out there again."

"Of course you can. Maybe one weekend we can all go."

"Out where?" Kylie asked.

"Rhodes End. Your dad was out there this week looking for arrowheads."

"Sounds like a plan. Daddy, the grill is ready and the steaks are on the counter."

"Got it." Carl walked away.

Kylie bumped LJ's hip. "Told you so."

Epilogue

LJ was sitting in her truck in the Aldridge driveway, her heart filled with trepidation and anticipation. "Can I do it?" She nodded, got out of the truck, and went to the front door, where she pressed the doorbell with her index finger.

The door swung open. "LJ, glad you could make it. Come on in." Carl stepped aside so she could enter.

"Did you make the reservations?" Virginia asked when she entered the kitchen.

"Yes. I was able to get a private room for just our party."

"Is everyone coming?"

"Yes. They were all excited to be there to celebrate her birthday."

"They know it's a surprise, right?"

"Yes."

"What did you tell her?" Carl asked.

"That Ryan and I were taking her out to celebrate." LJ grinned. "She thought Ruth's Chris Steak House was too extravagant."

"That is so like her." Virginia moved to the coffee machine. "Either of you want a cup?"

"Yes, please. I haven't had my quota for the morning yet." LJ moved closer to Virginia.

"I'm good," Carl said. "Where does she think you are now?"

"I told her I had a meeting. She was so engrossed in what she was telling the grad students that she didn't suspect a thing."

"I told her we unfortunately had a previous engagement with one of Carl's old Army buddies and we couldn't go to dinner with you, but I said I made a cake and hoped you all could stop by after dinner." Virginia handed LJ a full coffee cup.

"She won't be mad that we're surprising her, will she?" LJ took a sip.

"No, the last time we surprised her like this was on her sixteenth birthday. Remember that, Ginny? She loved it."

"Yes. She was smiling for weeks after that."

LJ nodded and gathered her courage. "I wanted to ask you both something," she began.

Virginia frowned. "Is something wrong?"

"No. Everything is fine." LJ reached in her pocket. "I wanted to ask your permission to marry Kylie." She took out a ring box and opened it.

It only took a moment for Virginia to wrap LJ in her arms. "Of course it is. A wedding. How wonderful."

Carl came over and put his long arms around both women. "You will make her even happier than she is now," he whispered.

Virginia looked at LJ with a twinkle in her eyes. "Does that mean we may have other grandchildren?"

LJ laughed. "I think you'll have to ask Kylie about that."

†

"I remember coming here years ago when Ted's office hosted a Christmas party. The food was wonderful but really expensive." Kylie began to open the car door.

"No, wait. Let me get that." LJ rounded the car, opened Kylie's door, and helped her out. "I'll get Ryan, and then we can go inside."

Kylie smiled when she saw the rich wood that accented the walls. She took in the wonderful smells that wafted around her. "This is too extravagant," she whispered to LJ, who was holding her hand. "We should go somewhere else."

"It's your birthday, and you are worth every penny."

"I don't think we're talking about pennies here." Kylie laughed.

"Dr. Evans. I have a six thirty reservation," LJ said to the hostess.

"Right this way."

When Kylie walked into the room, she heard people yelling "Surprise!" and saw her parents along with Granny Thorpe, Rob and his wife Louise, Lynne and her husband Tom, and Jodie and her husband Roger. She gasped. "Oh LJ, this is too much."

"Are you surprised?"

"Yes." She leaned into her. "I can't believe you did this for me," she whispered.

"I'd do anything for you, don't you know that?" LJ hugged her. "You deserve only the best, my love."

Soon everyone was sitting around a large round table,

digging into the appetizers before consuming their meals.

When everyone had finished dinner, Carl stood and smiled. "Before we have dessert, shall we open the gifts?" He winked at LJ.

Kylie had soon opened each present and treated each one as if it were a treasure. "I don't know what to say except thank you, everyone, for this wonderful night." She looked at the grinning LJ seated next to her. "Thank you so much for this surprise. It was totally unexpected and awesome of you to do it for me." She leaned in and kissed LJ's cheek.

LJ pushed back her chair, stood, and then bent down on one knee. "Kylie, you are the breath of my life, for no other love brings my life the meaning that you and Ryan do. Will you marry me?" She pulled the ring box out of her pocket, opened it, and held it out.

Kylie covered her mouth, and a tear escaped her eye. "Oh, yes, my love. Yes, yes, yes."

Everyone around the table began to clap as LJ slipped the diamond ring onto Kylie's finger.

With tears in her eyes, Kylie smiled. "This is the best night of my life." She looked at LJ and grinned. "Well, there may be one that was better," she whispered.

Not long after, Kylie's granny approached them.

"Granny, I'm so glad you could come." Kylie embraced her. "You being here makes this extraordinarily special day in my life all the more so." She held out her hand. "Isn't it beautiful?"

The older woman smiled and took LJ's hand in hers. "I have never seen Kylie so happy, and I know it's all because of you."

"Thank you, Mrs. Thorpe."

"Please call me Margaret." She held a gnarled finger up. "No, I think Granny is better."

"I'd be honored to call you that." LJ smiled. "I wish my gran was here. I think you two would have gotten along."

†

"Kylie," LJ whispered that night in their bed.

"Mm-hmm."

"I was thinking that maybe you, Ryan, and me could move out to the farm. It would be a wonderful place to raise children."

Kylie thought she was dreaming. She straightened up, and a glorious smile graced her face as she hugged LJ. "I love you."

LJ laughed. "I'll take that as a yes."

"How about yes, yes, yes! Can we have our wedding there?"

"That would be perfect. My grandparents were married there under that big oak tree in front of the house. According to my gran, the whole town turned out to celebrate the occasion."

"How about we just invite a few close friends?"

"Sounds like a plan to me. Are you happy?" LJ tried to tamp down her insecurities, but they wanted a voice.

"Deliriously so. Did you doubt that?"

LJ shrugged. "Not really. Bad habits are hard to break."

"I love you and can't wait to be your wife." Kylie kissed her. "When can we move? That will mean a longer drive to work. What about Ryan and school? There's so much to do...." Her eyes brightened. "LJ, did you say 'children'?"

LJ pulled Kylie in closer and kissed the top of her

head. "Yes, do you mind?"

Gray eyes misted over. "Oh, sweetheart, I want that with you. I want to have a family with you." She gently kissed LJ's lips and then opened her eyes wide. "LJ, we will have to add rooms to the house. Who will be the father? How many shall we have?"

Laughing, LJ shook her head. "My love, we can have as many children as you like. We will add on lots of bedrooms and fill them all."

"You're so wonderful. I love you so much. Can we move tomorrow?"

Bemused, LJ smiled. *She's like a dog with a bone and no thought of giving it up.* "Tomorrow might be a bit soon. How about within the next month?"

"Perfect." Kylie began kissing LJ in earnest.

How did I get to this point? A soon-to-be wife with a daughter and more children on a farm. "Hmm, Kylie, I'm not really keen on the idea of my having children. Do you mind?"

Kylie pulled back before wrapping her arms around the beautiful woman and kissing a bare shoulder. "Love, I can't imagine you pregnant. What do you say I do the baby thing?" Kylie leaned over LJ and picked up her phone off the nightstand.

"Kylie? Who are you calling...the sperm bank?" A rumble of laughter came from deep inside her as she spoke.

"No, I'm not calling them yet. I'm just getting the number so I can call in the morning. You know the father has to be tall and have blue eyes and black hair."

LJ took the phone and placed it back on the nightstand. Then she took Kylie in her arms and began kissing her. "What do you say we stop talking and I show you just how much I love you?"

Kylie giggled as she pulled the sheet up over their heads.

"Happy birthday, my love." LJ pulled her close, relishing the nearness of the woman she loved.

Late, into the early hours of the morning, their bodies entwined as their hearts, minds, and souls embraced in peace and love.

"LJ?"

"Mm-hmm?"

"I love you."

Then, in the hours just before dawn, LJ Evans smiled as her heart soared. "I love you too, baby." She thought of her grandmother, who had told her that love would sneak up on her one day and she'd be helpless to stop it from happening. *You were right, Gran. Right here in my arms is all I'll ever want or need.*

About the Author

Erin O'Reilly

Erin O'Reilly is an accomplished author with twenty-three published works, including her newest collaboration with JM Dragon *Take Me as I Am* and soon to be released *Ready for Love*. She was the Sapphic Readers Award winner for her book *Deception*. Her focus as a writer is to develop strong characters that make a dramatic impact on her story lines.

When not writing she is the technical Director and CEO of Affinity eBook Press. Contact Erin at erinoreilly@affinityebooks.com

Other Books from Affinity eBook Press

Neptune's Ring by Ali Spooner
In the sequel to *Venus Rising*, Nat and Liz, owners of Venus Rising, invite Levi and Vanessa to join them in a venture for a new club on another island. They find the perfect place in an unfinished resort Neptune's Ring. While on the island, Levi is drawn into a mystery involving secret compartments and a murder. Join the characters in this page-turning adventure, filled with steamy romance, intrigue and an unsolved murder.

The Ultimate Betrayal by Annette Mori
Lara is a successful, beautiful, charming, financier. She is also a total control freak, so whatever Lara wants, Lara makes sure she gets. Rachel is Lara's fun loving, charming, irresistible wife. Sophia's surprise visit to see Lara sets in motion a number of life changing events for them all. Hell has no fury as a woman scorned.

Keeping Faith by TJ Vertigo

Join the antics of Reece, Faith, Cori, Vi, and even The Animal, one last time in *Keeping Faith*. Faith has finally made the big screen, but how will Reece handle her success? Will the love that they share be enough to save their relationship and soothe The Animal?

Bound by Ali Spooner
A rogue master vampire threatens the existence of the New Orleans vampire clan. Lord Jordan enlists Devin Benoit, sister of the Baton Rouge Alpha, and her witch lover, Tia, to assist with cleansing the city from potential disaster.

The Circle Dance by Jen Silver
Jamie Steele has moved to another town, trying to forget the heartbreak of losing her lover of six years. Sasha Fairfield finds her thoughts taken up with her ex-lover and thinks she wants Jamie back. Follow this captivating romance as love dances through the lives of these women to its surprising conclusion.

Search for the White Moon by Natalie London
Kathryn Austin, a government agent, is given opera singer, Adriana Desi, as her new assignment. Their lives and futures are in danger as the White Moon terrorists hunt them. Immerse yourself in this fast-paced romantic thriller by debut author Natalie London.

Take Me As I Am by JM Dragon & Erin O'Reilly
When Jo Lackerly and Thea Danvers meet, an unexpected friendship develops, proving a catalyst for both women to change their lives irrevocably. Follow them on a journey of discovery that will have your heart smiling, blood boiling, and senses entangled in a wonderful romance.

Carved in Stone by Jen Silver
Join the characters from *Starting Over* and *Arc Over Time* in this final book from the Starling Hill trilogy. Ellie Winters thinks she might be going mad when the ancient queen wants a proper burial for herself and her consort. *Carved in Stone* has romance, adventure, a treasure hunt, and a happy endings for all, living and dead.

Anywhere, Everywhere by Renee MacKenzie
Gwen Martin's life in the Ten Thousand Islands area changes irrevocably when Piper Jackson comes into her life. Without trust, can the budding relationship between Gwen and Piper survive? Or will the answers to the questions continue to haunt them?

Venus Rising by Ali Spooner
Levi Johnson arrives at Venus Rising, an exclusive lesbian-only tropical resort in the Virgin Islands and finds more than she expected—a sizzling hot love triangle. Torn between her

attraction to two women, she struggles to choose the right woman to share her life.

The Devil's Tree by Ali Spooner
Torn between her love for the pack and her need to find what's missing in her life, Devin Benoit travels to New Orleans. Will the previous happenings at the Devil's Tree help or hinder Devin in the fight of her life, and the life of Tia, the woman who now owns her heart?

The Beggars' Coppice by Erica Lawson
Edda Case is a woman in crisis who discovers that things are not as they seem. Is it truly a message for her from beyond the grave or is something more sinister taking place? Can Edda solve the mystery of *The Beggars' Coppice*?

Locked Inside by Annette Mori
How much does the power of love matter to someone who must overcome obstacles far greater than most people face in a lifetime.

Line of Sight by Ali Spooner
Sasha and her lover Kara are back. Continue the thrilling adventures of this couple from the Sasha Thibodaux series.

Requiem for Vukovar by Angela Koenig

Requiem for Vukovar continues the Refraction series and the exploits of Jeri O'Donnell and her partner, Kelly Corcoran. In an epic siege largely ignored by the wider world, Kelly, who was prepared to give up comforts and certainties when she became part of Jeri's nomadic life, encounters more than physical danger. Her ability to maintain her core integrity is assaulted by the inevitable ugliness of war. For Jeri, the true battle is confronting her attraction to violence as she struggles against losing herself in the exhilaration of combat.

Against All Odds by JM Dragon
From award-winning and bestselling author JM Dragon, with significant updates by Erin O'Reilly, comes an original tale of romance where everything seems to be stacked against two women whose destinies bring them together. Life however takes a twisted path, setting both Steph and Louise in directions they never thought possible. Will love win out against all odds or will love be forever lost?

The Settlement by Ali Spooner
The outpouring of love and friendship toward Cadin helps her on her path to healing and learning to trust her heart to love once again. Join bestselling author Ali Spooner on this sensational journey that ends with a heartwarming romance.

Affinity
eBook Press
NZ

E-Books, Print, Free e-books

Visit our website for more publications available online.

www.affinityebooks.com

Published by Affinity E-Book Press NZ LTD
Canterbury, New Zealand

Registered Company 2517228